Feral

Mila Crawford

D1716007

Content Warnings

Dear reader this book contain some material that could be upsetting to some. Please proceed with caution. Your mental health is important.

Triggers

Violence and violent acts (Not against FMC)

Parricide

Talk of violence towards women and systemic violence.

Talk of religious abuse.

Child Abuse (off Page)

Content

MMMF

Degradation

Somnophilia

Capnolagnia

Primal

Spit play

Double Penetration including DVP

Knife Play

Blood Play

Gun Play

Fire Play

Breeding

Bondage

Breath Play

Praise

Pet Play

Snowballs

Fletching

Crawling/Begging

Grief can be the garden of compassion. If you keep your heart open through everything, your pain can become your greatest ally in your life's search for love and wisdom.

-Rumi

For anyone born in Iran after 1979. You deserved better.

Recipes

Gormeh Sabzi (Serve with Basmati Rice)

Ingredients

1 onion

4 cloves garlic

1 tsp turmeric

1 lb stewing meat

4 dried Persian limes

1/3 cup kidney beans, dried

4 cups fresh parsley, packed

2 cups fresh cilantro,packed

1 cup fresh feenigreek

2 cups fresh chives

salt & pepper

oil

Please note that for this recipe you will need to soak your beans for a few hours.

1. Dice onion and mince garlic. Sauté in oil until translucent . Add turmeric and stir well.

2. Cut meat in cubes and add to onion. Season with salt and pepper and allow to brown on all sides.

3. Make a couple of small holes in each of the dried limes. Add to the meat along with the beans. Add 4 cups of water, cover, and cook on medium for 1 hour.

4. In the mean time fine chop herbs.

5. Saute herbs in oil for a few minutes until you smell the aroma of the herbs. This is a very important step in making this recipe. DON'T skip this, it will make a difference in taste.

6. Add herbs to the meat and beans. Cook covered on medium low for 2 to 2 1/2 hours. Make sure to stir the pot every so often and also taste and adjust seasoning.

Shirazi Salad

Dressing: lime juice, salt and pepper, which you can whisk together before or just add when serving.

Ingredients

Persian Cucumbers

Roma Tomatoes

Red Onion

Fresh Parsley

1. De-seek the tomatoes for best results but this isn't neccessary.

2. Chop everything evenly and as small as you can. The smaller the pieces the better for the flavor.

3. Toss the salad immediatly before serving. This keeps it crunchy.

4. Adjust the seasoning with salt and pepper and lime juice as needed to your taste.

Playlist

Listen to the playlist Here

1. Heathens by Hailstorm

2. Dreams by The Cranberries

3. Upside Down by Jack Johnson

4. Float On by Modest Mouse

5. Steal My Kisses by Ben Harper and The Innocent Criminals

6. Chameleon Boy by Blue October

7. Hate Me by Blue October

8. Look After You by The Fray

9. Say it Right by Nelly Furtado

10. Shut Up And Drive by Rihanna

11. Fake Plastic Trees by Radiohead

12. Pump up Kicks by Foster The People

13. One Way or Another by Blondie

14. Firestarter by The Prodigy

15. Secrets by One Republic

16. Losing my Religion by R.E.M

17. Violet Hills by Cold Play

18. Perfect by Ed Sheehan

19. Talk by Hozier

20. Perfect by Ed Sheehan and Chance The Rapper

21. Another Love by Tom Odell

22. Would that I by Hozier

23. Granite by Sleep Token

24. Beraghsa by Mohsen Chavoshi

25. Soltane Gahlbha By Are

26. Haver Haver by Kourosh Yaghmaei

27. Flightless Bird by Iron and Wine

28. Starboy by The Weekend and Daft Punk

29. Ma Edame Darim by Hichkas

30. Maydooneh Hang by Toomaj

31. Ruff Ryders Anthem by DMX

32. Cyclone by T-Pain and Baby Bash

33. Falling to Pieces by Two Feet

34. River by Bishop Briggs

35. Fetish by Selena Gomez

36. Call out My Name by The Weekend

37. Mess is Mine by Vance Joy

Blurb

Ezekiel Summers, the son of a preacher, lost an eye because of me.

Cyrus Porter, the child of a sociopath, burned a man for touching me.

Levinston Cartwright, an heir to billions, used his wealth to stalk me.

Three vastly different, yet dangerous men with one thing in common...

An obsession with me.

Prologue

Azadeh — Age 29

THREE MONTHS AGO

The Manor

The concept of belonging can be many things to different people. For some, it's a ravenous crowd chanting their name and the allure of fame. Others gain accomplishment and abundance from the texture of green bills gliding between their fingers. For me, it's coming home to the three men who simultaneously comfort and obliterate me.

My gaze wanders to the lush forest surrounding Lev's property. I was surprised when he kept the place after his brutal and corrupt parents died. I didn't expect him to gut the interior and make it his permanent home, especially as it was the origin of tangible nightmares that continue to haunt him.

The bump against my shoulder pulls me from my reverie. "Penny for your thoughts?"

I turn my head, and a smile lifts my lips.

Ezekiel Summers. The boy who saved me and was "rewarded" with the loss of his right eye.

He grabs the cigarette mindlessly burning between my fingers and brings it to his lips.

I shove the pack of Marlboros toward him, smashing the pack against his chest. "You can have your own, you know."

Zeke inhales, and the tip lights up red. He doesn't say a word as he exhales the smoke. "I know, but this filter has been between your lips."

My face must turn every shade of red because Ezekiel chuckles and drapes his arm over my shoulders, pulling me toward him. Zeke's arms provide a sense of safety I rarely experience. For someone who survived one form of upheaval after another growing up, having a constant is a novelty not to be taken for granted.

A part of me regrets leaving, but I know if I don't, the seed of resentment will grow into a stubborn weed I'll never rid myself of.

We sit silently, sharing a cigarette, the act poignant in its intimacy. That's how it's always been with Zeke: friendship on the cusp of consuming passion. So many times, I wanted to say screw it and burn with him. Then I thought about all the stories I'd have to forgo to do it.

I glance at him as he looks into the darkness. The beautiful boy has transformed into a handsome man. Zeke was the boy who made me not hate men. He showed me what a man could be when he stood by you, protected you, and sacrificed for you. Zeke taught me that I could lean on someone and know that the trust I've given him would never be taken advantage of or abused.

But when it comes to telling him how he makes me feel, my throat dries up, and my mind becomes numb. I want to nestle in the safety of his arms for all eternity, but my need for comfort is constantly overshadowed by the girl who believes that if she embraces happiness, she's betraying her sisters, who have no choice but to reside in utter darkness.

The back door slides open, and I realize how safe I am with these three men. I don't need to be vigilant about my environment when they're with me. I smile, knowing Cyrus Porter is standing behind me by the flick of his zippo.

The three of us sit in silence, unsure of what to say or how to act, when a sulfurous odor suddenly assaults my nose.

Immediately, I turn to Cyrus. "Did you burn my hair?"

"No," he replies, trying to prevent the corner of his lips from turning into a smile.

"Are you gaslighting me?" I demand.

"I would never burn your hair, Az." Cyrus leans into me and whispers seductively, "You're one of the few people I'd only burn if you asked me."

I laugh. "That is a bald-faced lie because I can smell it."

I pull my hair over my shoulder and inhale, needing confirmation, before glaring at Cyrus. "You know I can smell it, right?"

"Consider it my version of a love bite. And we both know how much you love those love bites," Cyrus says as he wags his eyebrows.

4

It never fails to amaze me how attractive this man is, even with all the vicious scars covering half his face and the deep ridges burned into his skin. I know Cyrus has issues with them, covering what he can with blackout tattoos, but they're beautiful in their imperfections.

To many, Cyrus might be The Boogieman, but all I see is a sly smile and green eyes that remind me of freshly cut grass on a warm summer day. I love their beauty, but I've always loved things that cause others to turn away—my little menagerie of beautiful boys the world was too scared to love.

Cyrus winks as he hands me a black box neatly wrapped with a red ribbon before pulling a joint from his pocket and lighting it. Taking a few tokes, he stares out at the lush forest. He remains quiet, as if pondering something too complicated or painful to utter aloud.

"What's this for?" I ask, pulling him from his thoughts.

His cheeky smile returns. "Thought we'd have a little going away party."

I quickly rip off the bow and open the box, gawking at the contents. Nestled in black tissue are black panties and a bra. But this isn't just any lingerie. "The 9 Alarm Defender Briefs and sports bra?"

Cyrus exhales the smoke. "I like what I like, but I like your lady parts a little more, and I want to make sure they're protected."

I belt out a laugh before placing the box beside me.

"Whoa, are you turning your nose up at my thoughtful gift?" Cyrus demands, his bottom lip jutting with a pout. He yanks up the hem of his shirt, exposing his muscular chest, peppered with massive scarification and blackout tattoos like those covering his face. On the other side, my name is carved into the smooth, sun-kissed skin in jarring, jagged letters. "I think it's pretty shitty of you to allow me to partake in your crazy kink when you keep denying mine!"

I'm not sure when my fascination with knives started, but somewhere along the way, it consumed me. So much so that I began training with anything made of steel with a sharp pointed tip: swords, carving knives, boning knives, boot knives, skinning knives, universal knives, and gutting knives. My love for them also bled into a kind of depravity, increasing my appetite for sexual activities that included risk play. I became consumed with marking my lovers and tethering them to me in blood.

I glance at Zeke for backup, but he simply smiles, pulling up his shirt to display my name on his chest. "The only one who can't demand anything of you is Lev."

I huff. "It's not fair when it's two against one."

Zeke nuzzles his nose against my pulse point before growling in my ear, "Don't pretend you don't like it when we tag team you."

I'm suddenly hot, my skin burning. I have no idea why that happens. I wish I had a smart answer for lewd comments or flirting, but I've never been that girl. Which, in all honesty, makes no sense since I'm never at a loss for words. Yet every time my best friend takes our friendship to a sexual level, I stammer and fall apart.

"What's the matter, Princess? Cat got your tongue?" Zeke teases, nipping my ear and grazing his teeth along my delicate lobe. "I think you'd prefer it if I had your tongue instead."

I jump off the back steps, needing to put some distance between me and the heady scent of Ezekiel's cologne.

"Ah, come on, Hellcat." Cyrus smirks. "We've got all this space. I'd think you'd want to make use of it."

I frown at him, irritated by his mocking laughter.

Zeke gets up from the steps and stalks toward me. His body is lean and hard in all the right places. He brings the smoke to his lips, taking another drag, and I think about all the dirty things he's done to me with many cigarettes over the years.

I step backward. "What are you doing, Zeke?"

A twisted smile forms on Zeke's lips as he prowls toward me. "I was thinking about how hungry I am."

I point toward the back door. "The kitchen is that way."

Zeke laughs. "Come on now, Princess. You and I both know that's not the type of snack I'm craving."

I'm about to reply with a smart comment when Cyrus jumps off the porch and jogs over to Zeke. They both glare at me with predatory eyes as clouds of smoke shroud their faces. Zeke and I have played this game many times. One of us runs, and the other chases—our adult version of a child's game. But for the first time, Cyrus seems to want to play.

I arch my eyebrow and tilt my head at them, standing there in all their masculine glory. "I'm not sure I like my odds. Two against one isn't very sporting."

"Don't worry, Az. We both know Cyrus can't keep up. Think of him as a pity fuck."

Cyrus growls as he grabs Zeke's hips and tugs him until his back is flush with his chest. "That's not what you were saying when my cock was deep in your tight little ass. If I remember correctly, you were crying about how it was so fucking big. My favorite was when you screamed, 'Keep giving it to me, Daddy.'" Cyrus gyrates his hips, mimicking Zeke. "'Pound my little fuck hole. Make me feel so good, Daddy. Oh, Cyrus, that's it, I'm gonna come. Just like that.'"

Zeke wraps his arm around Cyrus's neck and flips him over, dropping him on the ground and holding him down with a booted foot. "Listen up, Cyrus. I've never called your punk ass Daddy, and I never will."

Cyrus laughs as his hand glides provocatively along Zeke's black army boot. "These are kind of hot. Maybe the next time I fuck your ass, I'll tie you up spread eagle, completely naked except for these. Legs in the air as you get fucked like the little bitch you are."

"When I shove my cock up your ass dry, you'll know who's the little bitch," Zeke spits.

I laugh at their insane banter. It's their foreplay. My guys love each other furiously, but they also fuck each other like mortal enemies. "Well, looks like you boys are busy, so I'll be going."

Both men turn their gazes on me as Zeke offers a hand to Cyrus and helps him up.

Cyrus lunges for me but misses as I sidestep. "You better run, Hellcat, because I'm hard as fuck and itching to punish your holes."

I smirk at my boys and dash into the forest. This isn't the first time I've run and been fucked in the forest. These games have always helped release the tension coiling in my veins. Running for pleasure and fun, not out of fear or vengeance. A welcome change of pace.

Leaves rustle and skitter behind me from two sets of feet belonging to two very determined men.

"When we catch you, Hellcat, I'm going to pound into that sweet pussy until you can't walk straight," Cyrus hollers from behind me.

"Gotta catch me first, Cy." I barrel through the forest, dodging low-hanging branches. I laugh as I glance behind me to see Cyrus huffing in pursuit.

"How the fuck are you so fast?" he wheezes, grabbing his chest.

"Perhaps you should sit this one out, Cy." Zeke chuckles as he runs past him, chasing me through the trees. "Let the big boy handle it."

Carefree laughter bubbles out of me. I'm always light around the guys. It's as if they possess magic, allowing all the troubles plaguing me to melt away. Moments like this make me want to stay, but then I remember that not all women experience what I have.

My world crashes around me as I contemplate the girls in Afghanistan and Iran and the girls in America sold to men who abuse them. I can only be with my guys in fleeting moments because I have important work to do. Those girls need me more than my boys.

My brother calls this bullshit survivor's guilt, and maybe he's right. But everything is down to chance first and choice second. I could've been a child bride sold by a desperate single mother who had multiple mouths to feed. I could've been born to a misogynistic man who believed that my life as a woman was meaningless. But I was lucky to be born to my mother, a woman who escaped oppression and braved the desert with three children.

"You've been practicing for a marathon," Zeke yells, humor lacing in his voice.

"Thought you said you were a big boy and could handle it," I holler back as I dodge a branch and jump over a shrub.

I glance behind me when Zeke doesn't retort with a smart comment. I don't see the guys and foolishly assume I've outrun or concealed myself for the moment. I turn to gain a greater advantage when I collide with a hard frame.

Zeke wraps his arms around me, turning me and holding me to his chest. His nose glides along my neck as he inhales audibly like an animal scenting me. "I said you got better, Princess. I never said you got better than me."

This is check, but it's not mate.

My feet lift off the ground, and I push back hard against Zeke's chest, giving him my full weight. He releases me as he stumbles, and I run.

"Gotta be better than that, Zeke. Your girl has been training with the best of the best in Jujitsu. I'm gonna revive the Hashashin."

Zeke laughs, and twigs snap behind me as he pursues.

I kick one of the trees, showing off the acrobatic wonder of the Asian martial arts I've learned over the years. My body swoops and dances with nature and the surrounding elements, demonstrating to Zeke and anyone else watching that I'll only be caught because I want to. My gaze darts around me, gauging where my boys might be. I'm startled when I glimpse the dark Italian wool of a gray three-piece suit and immediately stop in my tracks.

Lev.

He leans against a large elm tree, arms crossed over his broad chest. Wisps of black hair fall over his pretty gray eyes as he watches me. A regular old peeping tom.

Before I can say anything, I'm tackled onto the ground, and Zeke's deep voice rumbles, "Gotcha," in my ear.

I twist in the dirt below me, remembering the game as his beautiful face hovers above mine.

Zeke sniffs me again. "Fuck, you smell so good. Do you have any idea what it's like to get hard from someone's scent?"

It's immensely erotic when a man finds your scent so desirable he could lose his ever-loving mind. It's always been like that with Zeke. Even when we were kids, he made me feel like I was the center of his universe. This man, without even knowing me, came to my rescue. Zeke showed me it was possible to trust a man who wasn't my departed father or brother. Lying on the earth and gazing into his warm blue eye, I'm confident this man will never forsake me, no matter what I do. But I know I'm not ready to give him everything he deserves.

"How good?" I tease, wiggling beneath him as his hard, thick cock strains against me.

Zeke nips at my neck, sucking the delicate flesh and unleashing a lust to be marked by him. To wear his need and desire on my skin like armor, like a brand.

"Good enough to eat, baby," Zeke murmurs. "You always smell good enough to eat."

He works his way across my neck, kissing my face. Zeke always leads to aggression via tenderness. Guilt still lives within him, even after all these years. He worries that I'll resent him if he doesn't show me he loves me first. But I won't. I harbor only love and admiration for him.

I grab his face, forcing his eyes to mine. "I know you love me." I say the words with force and confidence. I don't want him to have any doubt that I need it hard, dirty, raw, and fast. "I'm safe here. You're safe here. We are safe here."

He nods before his lips brush the hollow of my neck, and he skinks his teeth into my flesh with a vicious desire. My screams amplify as his hand moves to my breasts, kneading them with violence and inflicting pain.

Zeke grabs my hair, yanking my head back to give himself better access. The sting on my scalp is an aphrodisiac, bringing me to new heights.

I'm so absorbed in our passion that I'm startled when a booted foot lands beside my head. Gazing up, I see Cyrus standing above me with a boyish grin. That smile would seem sinister to some people because of the severe burn marks on his face. But he's beautiful to me. My handsome jester with the broken heart. He's never outrun the little boy who did nothing wrong but was punished regardless.

The toe of Cyrus's booted foot scrapes along my cheek before he places it on my neck, restricting my ability to breathe. "You know what to do if it becomes too much. Blink twice if you understand."

I blink twice, informing him it's okay. That I am okay.

Cyrus nods. "Good fucking girl. Remember, Hellcat, we may fuck you like you're nothing but our dirty little whore, but you're the queen of our universe."

His words shower me like warm summer rain. I bask in the knowledge that these men call me whatever they want during sex because, time and time again, they've shown me the lengths they'll go to for me.

I sense the dirt he tracks across my cheek with the sole of his boot. An act meant to degrade me, but all it does is empower me. These three men could have anyone they wanted. Even with their scars and damage, they're perfect. To know I'm the only woman they've ever claimed fills me with pride and amplifies my desperate need for them. Realizing you've bewitched a man to where no one else will ever compare is a powerful drug.

Cyrus unbuckles his pants and unleashes his thick penis, hovering over me. He falls to his knees and taps my face with his long cock. "Open up, Hellcat. Show me how badly you want to be my filthy little slut."

My lips part, and with one full thrust, Cyrus hits the back of my throat, forcing me to gag. I relish the loss of control and the force with which he fucks my face. His taut ass is my only visual. Cyrus moans as I lap his shaft and a surge of power spikes inside me.

"That's it, baby. Show Daddy what a cock hungry whore you are, pretty girl. Look at how well you're choking for me. Such a good girl."

I love Cyrus's encouragement. I want to make him proud. I want to be the best in the world. A cock sucking gold medal-winning Olympian.

Shivers rack my body as he lifts my shirt, exposing my bare skin to the cool breeze. Zeke's teeth nip at me, his incisors puncturing my flesh. I lift my hips, in desperate need of relief any way I can get it.

Zeke chuckles between bites. "Such a greedy girl, Princess."

He grips my yoga pants and slides them off my body. His gentle hands are a contrast to his vicious teeth. The tip of his tongue glides along my skin until it meets the top of my panties. His hands move to my upper thighs, and he yanks my legs wide, bringing his nose to my center. He inhales again, tearing the cotton barrier between his mouth and my open, throbbing pussy with his teeth.

Zeke laps at me. "Such a perfect pink pussy." He sucks my clit, taking me deep into his mouth. "I should punish you, Princess. It's not fair to possess a cunt like this and keep it from me. I should tie you up so your pussy is open and ready for me to lick clean any fucking time I want."

Cyrus's enthusiastic thrusts muffle my moans. Drool drips from the sides of my mouth, and tears spring from my eyes as my breathing is restricted by his perfect balls covering my nostrils.

"Fuck, hearing you gag is the best sound on the planet. Even better than the screams of a man burning to death," Cyrus growls.

I laugh, causing myself to gag even more. To Cyrus, the sound is the equivalent of a Shakespearean love sonnet.

"You know, Lev, if you got the stick removed from your asshole, you could fuck like a normal person instead of standing on the sidelines with your dick in your hand," Cyrus says.

I turn my head, and my eyes connect with Lev's. He's fixated on me and the scene before him, hands in his pockets. It's a position I've seen many times before: the lurker witnessing an erotic scene he desperately wants to partake in but can't.

I extend my arm, inviting him to join us, but he simply shakes his head. For years, I blamed myself for Lev's actions. Maybe he didn't want me, or maybe the idea of sharing me with the guys upset him. But I realized neither was true. Lev couldn't be with anyone because he couldn't bear to be touched.

I stare at the tattoos along his neck, knowing those markings trace every inch of his skin. I asked him once why he allowed a tattoo artist to touch him when he denied me. His answer was simple. "They never touch me. Not in the ways it matters. Their touch causes a numbing pain, not pleasure or something even deeper. Love."

Cyrus pulls out of my mouth, and I gasp for air. I watch as he shoves off his boots, followed by his jeans. He bends and rifles in the side pocket, pulling out a small bottle of lube. Turning to me, he smiles and waves the bottle in the air. "Never know when you're gonna have a quickie in the woods."

I burst out laughing, appreciating his timing. Cyrus might not always be appropriate, but he provides comic relief when the weight of life pulls me down. Zeke is my anchor, but Cy is my flotation device. My backup if things go wrong. And Lev is the turbulent ocean that draws me in but threatens to drown me.

"I'm gonna fuck you raw, Hellcat. Use all your holes and turn you into a communal cum dump. I'll come so deep in your big, sexy ass, and once you're filled to the brim, I'll watch you walk back to the manor as I leak down your legs." Cyrus walks around me, gripping Zeke's hair and pulling him off me before crashing his mouth to Zeke's to taste me on his glistening lips. They pull apart, and Cyrus's eyes flutter shut as he circles the tip of his tongue around Zeke's lips. "You taste so good, Hellcat. But you'll taste even better with multiple hot loads inside you."

Zeke smirks and grips my hips, flipping me over. I squeal as I brace my palms on the cold ground. All I can see is the dirt beneath my face and Zeke's army boots.

"Make yourself useful, Cyrus, and pull down my pants," Zeke demands.

I close my eyes in anticipation and focus on the slide of Zeke's leather belt and the rasp of his zipper.

Zeke groans as the tip of his cock presses against my entrance. "You're a good girl, Azadeh. My fucking princess. But I'm about to punish this pussy as if you've been very bad."

Zeke's fingers dig into my calves, holding me up while his cock mercilessly thrusts into me. I'm stretched to the brim, but I savor the pinch of pain from his massive girth. It feels good. It allows my brain to shut off and focus solely on the sex. On them. My boys.

Firm hands spread my ass open, and a tongue delves into my anus. The sweep of Cyrus's warm, wet tongue is oddly relaxing, contradicting the brutal assault of Zeke's dick in my pussy.

"I could eat this fucking ass forever and still want more," Cyrus mumbles between licks and swirls of his tongue. "I'm gonna suck all my cum out once I fill it. Taste that sweet ass mixed with my jizz."

Cyrus doesn't move his tongue as cold liquid hits my ass. He doesn't use his fingers to spread the lube around my asshole. Instead, he dips his tongue further into my anus. I remember the first time he did this, how uncomfortable and unsure I was about it all. Let's just say sexual repression is prevalent in Iranian culture. It doesn't matter what religion you're raised in or how forward-thinking your parents may be. I had to get past that little hump to truly explore my sexuality and indulge my passions. It helped that I was with men who didn't believe in societal norms or conventions, men who pushed and pushed until all my boundaries and hang-ups vanished.

Once Cyrus is done with his tongue, he uses the pad of his thumb to push as much lube as possible into my ass. Then he works his thumb in, distributing the lube evenly before slapping my ass. "I love fucking this juicy ass. It's fucking big and sexy. And I love how these cheeks jiggle for me. If you ever lose your ass, I'm gonna be one pissed-off man."

He lines up his cock with my anus and pushes in slowly, giving me time to adjust. Once he's comfortable that I can take him, he thrusts in rhythm with Zeke, manipulating my body to the brink of ecstasy.

My legs shake as Zeke presses his thumb to my clit, making circular motions that add to my pleasure.

"Look at how well you're taking us, Princess," Zeke coos. "Such a good girl, getting nice and stretched for us. I feel Cyrus in your ass, baby. It makes your tight pussy even more impenetrable. You like being used by us, don't you, baby?"

My pussy leaks more lubrication as their filthy mouths pull me closer to the edge. Dirty talk is an art, and more men need to learn how to do it. The added euphoria of verbal stimulation is the engine of the car.

I hear footsteps, and another pair of feet pause by my head.

"If you aren't gonna join us, make yourself useful and spit on that puckered little asshole," Cyrus taunts Lev.

A moment of silence. Then Lev spits.

Cyrus chuckles. "That's it, Lev. Be a good boy, and lube us up. Take out your dick. I can see the outline straining against your pants. I'd offer to blow you once I'm done here, but you don't like that, do you?"

I can't see if Lev has taken Cyrus's advice or if he's watching the scene with a scowl. But I also don't care because my entire body spasms as an earth-shattering orgasm blasts through me.

"That's it, baby. Come for us," Zeke encourages as he fucks me with greater force. "I love how your little pussy grips my dick as you come around it. Such a good girl. You got another for me, Princess?"

Cyrus and Zeke continue to fuck me, but Zeke's thumb is no longer on my pussy. Instead, it's replaced with a tongue. It's not possible for either man to fuck me and eat me out. They're pretty flexible, but not *that* flexible.

"That's it, Lev. Lick her up like a good boy. Show our pretty little slut how much you like eating her cunt. Let your tongue do what you refuse to do with your dick."

Lev? He's never done this before. I knew Zeke was working with him on his aversion, but I never thought he'd be at this level. Then again, I assume he isn't touching any other part of me.

"Don't you dare stop what you're doing, Lev," Zeke orders. "Lick that pretty pussy until your mouth is covered with her. Her cunt likes it. She's tightening for me. Our girl is gonna cum on your face, Lev."

"Bro, he's going nuts. I think he enjoys eating pussy more than you do," Cyrus says.

I have to agree with Cyrus because Lev's tongue laps me like a cat with a bowl of milk.

Within minutes, my legs stiffen, and another orgasm racks my body.

"Fuck, I'm gonna come," Cyrus and Zeke growl simultaneously as they release within me.

Zeke grips my ankles and lowers me to the ground as both men pull out. "You want your reward, Lev?"

"That's *my* fucking prize," Cyrus says with a childish pout.

"Move her to the tree, Zeke," Lev demands.

I gaze at Zeke. For a second, I think he'll say no. Zeke isn't a pushover, and the guys can never get him to do something he doesn't want to do. On the surface, Lev would seem to be the boss, but in reality, it's Zeke. He has a way of ensuring obedience, and his gentle authority is something most people easily dismiss.

A smile forms on Zeke's lips as he yanks me up like a leaf floating in the wind rather than a two-hundred-pound woman.

I gaze at Lev as Zeke braces me against the tree.

Lev tugs his belt from its loops with one pull as he walks toward me. "Pull her arms behind the tree trunk."

"Remember your safe word. If it's too much, say the word, and it's over, got it?" Zeke reminds me.

"I'm fine," I whisper. I won't say that word until I'm so broken that I think I might die. I'll let Lev do anything he wants to me because in all the years I've known him, this is the closest he's ever come to being a part of us, at least physically.

Zeke pulls my arms back and wraps them around a narrow tree, gripping my wrists. Cool leather wraps around my flesh, holding me in place.

Lev walks around the trunk and glares at me.

I lift my chin challengingly. "Am I supposed to stand here naked for your viewing pleasure, or did you have something else in mind?"

"How does it feel, Azadeh?" Lev asks, his voice cold.

"How does what feel?" I retort.

"How does it feel to know you have three men waiting at home pining for you while you galivant around the globe?"

"I don't know," I spit. "Why don't you ask the men who've done that for centuries? Or how about you talk to the women who sit at home raising children while their husbands get up to all kinds of things they shouldn't?" I smile as Lev's jaw ticks. "Besides, Lev, I never asked you to wait for me. Live your life. Be free. No one's holding you down."

Lev steps toward me. "I don't like wanting things I can't have."

I'm pissed. I want to kick his ass and pin him beneath me with a knife at his throat. I want the upper hand and don't enjoy that he's in a position to gain it. I smirk and sing "You Can't Always Get What You Want" by The Rolling Stones.

Cyrus slaps his ears with his palms. "How the fuck can someone so hot sound like a goddamn dying cat when she sings?"

Lev and I ignore Cyrus's outburst as we face off with each other. I'm about to goad him again when he steps closer. Enough to feel his hot breath on my skin as he leans forward, but not enough to touch me.

"I want to do ungodly things to you—things a man shouldn't do to a woman he loves. I want to hear you beg for mercy and promise you'll do anything to make it stop. That's not normal, Az. I'm not fuckin' normal. What kind of man wants to tear apart the person he loves the most to watch them bleed?"

I shrug. "I don't know. What kind of woman carves her initials into the men she loves? My purpose in your life is not to judge you, Lev. You understand my boundaries. I trust you'll stop if I tell you. You have urges and desires that most don't deem palatable, but it doesn't mean you're not a good man. What's good anyway? I grew up in a world where supposedly religious men raped fourteen-year-old girls because killing a virgin was unforgivable in the eyes of God. The three of you had fathers who were praised by strangers while they tortured their sons. They might not deem the four of us good or proper because we've had to do questionable things to protect innocence, but fuck them and fuck that. The only thing that matters is we accept you. I accept you. But most importantly, I trust you.

Do your worst, Lev. I'll still love you in the morning."

Lev's jaw twitches and his eyes catch fire. For a moment, I think this is it. Lev is finally letting us in. Then he lowers his eyes and walks away, leaving me tied to the tree with Zeke and Cyrus's cum dripping from my crevices.

"Is that it? You're gonna run away again?" I call after him, trying to free my hand from the makeshift shackles. Anger rises, and I long to lash out. "You're a good man, Lev. But you know what else? You're a fuckin' coward."

Lev stops in his tracks and turns his head to me. I think he's about to say something, but then he's in front of me in a flash, his gun pressed to my temple. "I'm not good, Az. There's nothing good about me. I like guns, I enjoy violence, and I'm obsessed with you. Nothing about me being with you will turn out well."

I inhale a sharp breath as he drags the barrel of the gun along my body, circling my nipples before moving it between my breasts to the top of my mound.

He lowers the gun. "You're right. I'm a coward, Azadeh."

My legs part unconsciously, my body screaming with fear and excitement.

Zeke steps forward while Cyrus jerks his cock like a dog who's seen a tantalizing piece of meat. I shake my head, warning Zeke to stay back.

My logical mind screams at me to say my safe word because this has gone too far, too quickly. But the girl who likes danger and craves fear holds her breath, anticipating what comes next.

Lev rubs my clit with the barrel of the gun, moving lower until the tip presses against the entrance of my pussy. "Taking a chance on me is like being fucked by this gun." He pushes the barrel inside me until it's in all the way, a crazy smile on his lips as he fucks me with it slowly. "We're both loaded. You never know if or when we'll go off."

"I live for danger," I whisper, arching my hips toward him. "But I'm also a vengeful bitch. Know this, Lev; one day, you'll crawl like a dog for me to fuck you this way." When he arches an eyebrow, I lock eyes with him. "Remember, you gifted me the other gun that goes with this pair."

Lev's nostrils flare, and I know I have him. His lizard brain is front and center, and right now, he isn't thinking about anything other than fucking me. I have all his focus. He moves his hand vigorously, fucking me hard and deep with the metal barrel. Fear spikes in my veins, knowing that this lack of control could end with a bullet lodged in me, but I don't care. All I want is for my Lev to loosen up, to live, to experience something, *anything* other than his self-imposed misery.

"That's it, Lev. Make me come," I encourage. "Show me exactly what a gun worth over two million dollars can do."

Zeke and Cyrus move toward us. Zeke sucks a nipple into his mouth and the other between his fingers. He bites and pinches, adding an element of pain that brings me close to the edge. Cyrus sits between my legs, lifting me as his tongue lashes my asshole, sucking out the cum he recently deposited there.

"Don't leave," Lev pleads.

"I have to. People depend on me," I whimper as I come undone, my body trembling with another release.

Lev pulls out his gun and brings the barrel to his mouth, wrapping his lips around it and licking it clean of my juices. When he's confident he's savored every inch of me off the metal, he places it back in the holster at his side and gazes at me. "We depend on you too, or do we not matter?"

With that, he turns and walks away.

Chapter 1

Azadeh — Age 29

Present Day

"There will be many challenges in life. Some will propel you forward, while others will kick you with such force that you will believe you'll never recover from them. But if you remember one thing, you will never falter. Family is everything, Joonam. Never forget that."

My mother's words are a mantra playing on an endless loop in my mind.

Family is everything.

All I've done for the last six years is run from my family. Instead of being at home with the people I love, I've been galivanting all over the globe, helping strangers.

I bang the steering wheel with my open palm, needing to break something or myself. The grief and regret simmering inside me are at boiling point.

The road in front of me becomes a blur as thoughts of my dead mother ravage my mind, taking over like a virus that leaves nothing behind. An ironic smile forms on my lips as I ponder her words about feminine energy.

Never forget that it was women who led the Persian Immortals.

My mother was a juxtaposition. A strong, independent woman raised in the brutal bonds of religious patriarchy. She had a thirst for knowledge and a desire to demolish the chains that held her in place. From a young age, she read us stories about strong Persian women: Grand Admiral Artemisia, Irdabama, and Atrunis, amongst others.

Don't let a man dictate your worth or your capabilities.

My mother sang the virtues of independence and forging your own path, but she was also concerned about the opinions of neighbors who didn't know or care about her. That part of her essence was based on the bullshit purity culture that the government of Iran doused her with like a baptism. Though her struggles with the patriarchy were something she could never sever, my mother ensured that all three of her children could.

Nasrin Baran was a single mother who escaped persecution after witnessing her thirteen-year-old daughter receive seventy-two lashes following the public execution of her husband. Those two traumatic events forced her to push past and strive daily to shatter the ties to a country she both loved and despised in the same breath. Those encounters with religious patriarchal systems meant my mother constantly checked her gender biases and allowed her children to be who they wanted to be rather than the contrived "ideals" of corrupt men.

My mother was a pioneer. Her struggle and sacrifice gifted me with my freedom. For that, I will forever be grateful.

At thirty-eight, Nasrin packed up her three children—the youngest was nine—and walked away from the only home she'd ever known in the dead of night. Forced to deal with shady men and potential slaughter while she prayed to a god she believed might have abandoned her for the deliverance of her family.

My mother wasn't a warrior, nor was she a woman of means or luxury. Nasrin Baran lived in a desperate situation that forced her to be a survivor. Because of her struggle, she ensured her son and two daughters became no one's victim.

Memories of my mother don't plague me like they used to. Over the years, I've learned to compartmentalize the different facets of her identity.

A frightened newcomer who didn't want to offend anyone by taking up space.

The Protector who loved her children with an unrivaled ferociousness.

A mature student who grappled with self-imposed shame rather than prideful perseverance when she had to get recertified after being at the top of her field as a nurse in Iran.

The perfectionist in her also demanded it from her children.

I didn't bring you to America so you could turn into garbage. A B-plus is not what my sacrifices were for.

She was an immigrant who was grateful for America but never gave up on the idea of seeing home.

One day, Iran will be better. We will show the world what it means to be the descendants of Cyrus the Great. Our people are merciful and strong. We've survived it all, and this, too, shall become a footnote in our long history. When we go home, Azadeh. I'll show you the Aladaglar Mountains.

She'd pull me to the computer, and we would wait patiently for images of the rainbow mountains to pop up on the screen. But no matter what part of herself she showed to the world, my mother continuously proved through her actions that a woman was the captain of her destiny—she simply needed to be brave enough to grasp it.

She never got to go home. Nasrin Baran died in an American hospital, leaving three young adult children to pave a path for themselves.

I blink back tears as the manor house comes into view. I haven't seen my men for three months. I've missed them. But one of them has betrayed me. And I intend to have my vengeance.

Chapter 2

Zeke   Age 15

High School Cafeteria

"Do you even speak English?" Courtney Paulson asked while shoving the new girl into the cafeteria.

The teacher said her name was Azadeh. I wasn't sure how to pronounce it. Sounded pretty, though, like her. I also liked her hair. It was black or very dark brown and fell in loose springs down her back to her butt. It was shiny but not in the greasy way that some people's hair was. Azadeh's hair shined like the stars in the midnight sky. Was that a thing? I didn't know, but I had an overwhelming urge to rub the strands between my fingers.

"Maybe she doesn't know how to speak." Rachel Kilterson smirked.

I wished Rachel didn't know how to speak. The girl had the most annoyingly nasal voice on the planet.

"Why does she smell like that?" Kathy Markson sneered.

Kathy Markson should talk. She farted once in the second grade, and it was like a three-month-old fish curled up with a carton of rotten eggs.

I tensed as the three girls performed their vulture dance around their defenseless prey. This wouldn't end well. I knew these girls were petty and ruthless. They'd cultivated a hierarchy that put them at the top of the pecking order, thanks to the help of their insufferably rich parents. Parents who had indulged their every whim, even at the expense of innocent bystanders.

I gripped the table, knuckles white as I witnessed the verbal abuse of the new girl. I stayed out of it while the decrepit crows limited their torment to gawking. But when they smashed her modest meal to the floor, their mocking laughter bouncing off the cafeteria walls, I was out of my seat and in front of them in four quick strides. I was prepared to fend off Azadeh's tormentors before they created more carnage.

"Leave her alone, Courtney," I demanded.

Courtney stared at me, eyes rounded and mouth wide in utter shock. I guessed her reaction made sense. I rarely spoke to anyone at the school, and when I did, it was because I had to. My days were spent suffering through classes with the simpletons and vermin of the world until the hours ticked by, and I finally got to go home. So I understood why my actions were out of the norm for Courtney and her coven of witches.

Rachel's mouth twisted in disgust. "Why do you care about this... thing?"

"Maybe it's not about her," I growled. "Perhaps I'm sick and tired of the way you three bitches torment every fuckin' human being that you perceive as beneath you." I stepped toward Rachel until her back hit the cafeteria table. "I suggest you and your band of merry bitches pack it up and leave Azadeh alone."

"Or what?" Courtney asked. Her long, manicured neon green nails gleamed as she placed her hands on her hips.

The corners of my lips curled up. "You know who my grandfather is, don't you, Courtney? You've heard the rumors about how he tortured his victims for hours on end, cut up their bodies into various pieces."

One of Courtney's hands slid off her hip to hang at her side, and she took a step back. With the other hand, she gripped the back of Kathy's shirt, pulling her away from me and abandoning Rachel to the brunt of any unhinged act I might commit.

Ignoring the cowards, I turned my gaze to Rachel, wanting to ensure she was as terrified as the other bitches. "They say the shit my grandpa did is genetic." I leaned forward, whispering so that only Rachel would be privy to my words. "You'd make a pretty first victim."

Through all this, Azadeh remained seated. Her long dark hair fell like curtains around her face. She was visibly shaking, but she didn't move. I didn't like that she appeared so frightened and didn't understand why.

I bent slowly so I didn't spook her more than I already had. Maybe it was because I knew what being the new kid was like. But for Azadeh, it seemed somewhat worse because not only was she at a new school full of assholes, but she was also in a new country, away from everything familiar.

I sat across from her and smiled to put her at ease. I was sure I appeared like a crazed psycho. She just heard me talk about being a killer, and then all I did was smile at her. Azadeh lifted her head, peering at me through her pretty hair.

I jabbed my finger to my chest. "I'm Ezekiel, but you can call me Zeke."

She pointed to her chest. "Azadeh. English no good, but learning. Nice meet you, Ze-eck."

Usually, I wanted to bust someone's lip for fucking up my name, but she could've called me a hot pile of shit, and I would've been happy as long as it meant she kept talking to me. I wanted to know everything about her.

"Your name is beautiful."

She blushed and averted her eyes. "Thank you. Means free."

"You speak a language other than English?"

Azadeh nodded. "Yes, Persian."

"Persian like the cat?"

She laughed at my question, and I swear I saw angels appear. Okay, not really, but I wouldn't be shocked if they did.

"Yes, like cat. Me from Iran."

"Oh, cool. I went to Los Angeles with my father a few years ago, and there's a big Iranian community there. Y'all have killer food."

"Killer?" Her back straightened, and a frown furrowed her brow. "No, our food no kill. We not killer. Like here, good people and bad people. But we

mostly good, like Americans. Our government bad, like yours."

I hated seeing the panic in her eyes. Her hands moved expressively, and her face scrunched up in frustration, which made me realize she was searching for words she couldn't grasp.

I touched her arm, an action I regretted when she immediately pulled away. "Azadeh, no. I meant the food is good." I rubbed my stomach in circular motions. "You know it tastes good. I like the food."

Azadeh took a breath, and her shoulders dropped. Her face broke into the most radiant smile I'd ever seen.

"I liked that meat dish. Long piece of ground beef with yellow rice. That was so good. Puts American BBQ to shame, I'll tell you that."

Her smile grew. "Kabob. It's also my favorite. We not have BBQ but my maman makes it in oven. Tomorrow, you come my house for dinner. We cook Kabob for you. To say thank you for helping today."

I smiled. "I'll go anywhere you want. Tell me where and when."

Chapter 3

Zeke   Age 29

Present Day

Cyrus moans, shoving his head under the pillow as I step out of the shower. "Bro, get some fucking therapy for your sleeping habits. Getting up before the sun rises is fucked up."

I slap Cyrus's naked ass. "Keep flapping your mouth, and I'll wake you up by shoving my cock down your throat."

"You promise?" Cyrus wags his eyebrows.

My gaze roams his muscular frame covered in vicious burn marks. They trail in intricate swirls from his left arm across his chest and up the left side of his face. Bending, I trace my tongue along the indented flesh of his thigh until I get to his hard cock, pointing straight to the ceiling.

Cyrus fists his hand in my wet hair as he pulls me closer to the tip of his dick. "You know if you wake me up like this, my ass will become a morning person too."

I open my lips wide and take his girth into my mouth, pushing my head down until he hits the back of my throat. My tongue glides around his smooth shaft as I gag from the upward motion of his hips, causing his cock to move deeper.

Cyrus and I move in rhythm until his body goes still. He holds my head down firmly, and I gag again as he fills my mouth with his cum. I close my eye and swallow the load he's given me, and his hands loosen around my head.

"Guess you won't be needing that protein shake now." Cyrus wipes a drop of cum from the side of my mouth with his index finger before sucking it clean.

I smirk as I drop my towel and rummage for jogging pants and a t-shirt.

"Whoa, what's the rush? Thought we'd hit up rounds two and three."

I turn to witness Cyrus pointing to his dick, which is raring to go again. My lips curve at his ostentatious nature, and I shake my head. Usually, I'd be on him, flipping him over as I sink my teeth into his flesh and fuck him raw, but the marks on his body from last night need to heal. Guilt hits me as I glance at the teeth marks and fresh bruises on his flesh, some on his unmarked skin, while others are prominent on his scars.

"You still gotta heal from last night. I was pretty rough on you."

Cyrus spits on his hand and smiles as he glides it over his shaft, pumping it slowly. "Fuck, yes, you were, but that Epsom salts bath with jasmine helped.

"Gotta thank Azadeh when she finally decides to come home," I say as I pull the black cotton t-shirt over my head.

"If she ever comes home," Cyrus whispers, staring wistfully at the ceiling.

The clown is somber as he realizes he misses her. We all miss her. She hasn't been back in months. Her absence has done things to our psyche we can't explain, each of us coping in our fucked-up way. Some coping mechanisms are healthy, some questionable, and others downright destructive. I'm not sure why Azadeh has stayed away this long, but the ache in my heart won't quit. I want to track her down, bring her back against her will if I have to.

I've learned over the years that Cy needs space when he's solemn. Solitude helps to center him in ways I can't. At first, I found it odd since he played the jester. But over the years, we've created a solid bond that allows him to express his wants and needs. A bond I hope Lev will also be a part of.

I kiss Cyrus's head before leaving him in the room to wallow in misery.

Downstairs, I find a pot of coffee already started. Lev must've had an early start. I pour the hot liquid into a plain black mug and stare out the window.

There's always a vacancy when Azadeh isn't here. The three of us continue our lives and even find joy in our activities, but something is always lacking.

Jaheh shoma Kahliheh.

Over the years, Azadeh and her family have taught me Farsi. At first, I learned the language to communicate with her since she was learning English. But over time, I appreciated the poetic nature of the tongue and how everything was an emotive arrow straight to the truth of things. In Persian, you don't simply say, "I miss you." You say, "Jaheh shoma Kahliheh," which means your place is empty. Azadeh not being here has left a void that nothing and no one can ever fill.

I walk out to the front of the house and sit under the pretty little gazebo built for Azadeh —a gazebo she's never sat in. She told Lev it would look beautiful facing the willow trees.

Mornings bring solace. Sipping a cup of coffee and puffing on a smoke in the butt fuck hours of dawn brings a sense of peace and solitude. If I could capture the mist before the sun comes up and live in its essence forever, I would.

I used to despise this hour of the day. When I was younger, there was a forced obedience to it. Mornings were a time for prayer. Cleanliness in order to communicate with the big man upstairs and thank him for my abusive dad and robot mom. The irony of forcing a little boy to praise the lord for providing a sperm donor who gave him a black eye and fractured ribs.

I close and open my eye, trying to force the images of my past to dissipate like the smoke from my cigarette. I've been good at shoving my childhood trauma in a box and ensuring the lid stays on tight, but occasionally that shit sneaks up and bites me in the ass. But living with that man taught me how to mask my fucked-up desires. People would never assume I'm capable of the most horrendous acts known to man.

I take in the vast landscape before me, the manicured lawns and enormous trees with cascading branches lining a long driveway that ends at a majestic iron gate.

We didn't want to live here originally. It was meant to be a pit stop before Lev, Cyrus, and I figured out our shit. But as they say, life happens when you're busy making other plans. One thing led to another, and the manor became a refuge of sorts. A prison of our own making to complement the prison where we met.

Of the three of us, I figured it would be Lev who wouldn't want any part of this place—a stark reminder of hell and insanity. I realized how fucked up Lev was the day he gutted his parent's room and moved into it. The same room where he bashed his mother's head in with a Victorian bust. I suppose we all deal with our parental drama in different ways.

I take a haul of my smoke before sipping from the ceramic mug, relishing the burn of the scalding coffee coating my throat. My eyesnarrow as a black two-door sports car stops at the gate. The door to the sleek black machine opens, and I instinctively reach for my eye patch. Losing my eye was the worst thing that ever happened to me.

Stepping out of the vehicle is the girl who cost me my eye but gave me a family. Azadeh Baran.

The patio chair shifts, and black coffee spills on the table as I rush to my feet and sprint to the gate like a dog excited to see its owner after a long day. This is how it's always been with Azadeh and me. She goes off to discover new things, and I wait to welcome her home.

Maybe that's one of the reasons the three of us kept this house. We made excuses that it was convenient or the layout of the manor and the land around it were so massive that it could shelter us from our seedy activities. But we all knew why we stayed frozen in time. It was so a pretty girl with long black hair always had a place to call home.

Azadeh gets back in the car as the gates swing open, granting access to the sleek black Maserati. I'm uncertain if I should keep running toward her or have some dignity and let her drive to me. Logically, the cool thing to do is to act aloof and wait. But when it comes to Azadeh, I've never had any chill. There's something magnetic about her. A wild rose you want to encase in glass so you can gaze at its wonder for all eternity.

My decision is made when the car comes to a halt beside me. The engine's roar is silenced, and Azadeh storms out of the car.

Before she can say anything, I've wrapped my arms around her in a bear hug as I twirl her in the air. Azadeh Baran. My girl looks good. Better than good. She nuzzles her head in the crook of my neck, and my cock instantly hardens. She's the only girl who's ever been able to pull that voodoo. My skin lights on fire when she brushes her lips against my flesh.

Fuck, I missed her. I knew my relationship with her would never be more than fleeting moments because of her ambition, but she stayed away far too long this time.

"Look what the cat dragged in. About time you stopped by during your world tour, Princess. I know everyone needs saving, but your three men have missed you desperately."

"I've missed you too, Zeke. So damn much, but this is going to have to wait." Azadeh pulls away from me, and I notice her tired, red-rimmed eyes. She glances at the manor and clenches her teeth. "Where's Lev?"

I place her down and look her over. Her arms hang by her sides, her hands clenching and unclenching, her stance rigid as if she's hankering for a fight. Lev and Azadeh have always managed to get under each other's skin, pushing buttons left and right until one explodes in anger. But never in all these years have I witnessed her wanting to rip his head off his torso and place it on a spike. Until now.

"Did he do something?"

There's no way Lev would hurt her. He loves her.

Azadeh pushes past me and runs to the front door. Like the dutiful puppy who senses his owner is upset, I chase after her, coming to a halt before Azadeh opens the front door and busts into the foyer.

"Get your ass out here, Lev!"

"Hello, Az," Lev says, emerging from his office. He's wearing his typical three-piece suit, all prim and proper, giving the illusion of a refined businessman. Yet the ink peeking from his crisp cotton shirt collar and the words "fuck" and "life" tattooed on his knuckles tell a different story. Lev tugs at the lapels of his light gray suit jacket as if he's been inconvenienced by the help before settling his gaze on Azadeh. "Welcome home."

Azadeh doesn't say anything. She looks at Lev as if she wants to rip his flesh from his bones and stomp on his discarded remains. In the years I've known Azadeh, I've never seen her glare at one of us with such disdain and venom. When her claws are out, it's usually because she's digging them into our backs and begging to be fucked harder.

Before I can stop her, she bulldozes toward Lev, and a loud slap reverberates in the hallway, echoing off the cathedral ceilings.

"How could you?" she shrieks. "I thought you gave a fuck about me. You were working on your shit, Lev. Zeke was helping you. I believed that no matter how insane you behaved, you would always have my back. How could you?"

"Whoa, what the fuck is going on?" I demand.

Azadeh knows not to touch Lev unless he initiates it. We all know that. Lev's jaw ticks as he rubs the red mark marring his skin. I'm not sure if I'm more worried about Azadeh or Lev. Either could blow.

Azadeh turns to me, voice shaking from the tears I know she's trying to hold at bay. She's always been worried about appearing weak. Crying gives her enemies the upper hand and exposes her wounds. "Were you in on it?"

Azadeh is substantially more unhinged than Lev at the moment. I raise my hands, palms open wide. "I don't even know what's up. Whatever you're mad at him for, it has nothing to do with me. I swear it on my good eye."

Azadeh squints as she stares me directly in that good eye, assessing me, deciding if I'm being honest or pulling her leg.

"Az, I fuckin' sacrificed an eye for you. You think I'd ever do anything to hurt you?"

She tilts her head and glares at me with her rich brown eyes. Fuck, I love those eyes. They're so damn expressive, always telling on her even before her mouth opens. Those eyes made me jump to her rescue all those years ago. I still remember the first time I saw her, a scared little mouse hurled into a new world where she didn't know anyone or understand anything.

Her eyes are still fixed on me as if she's deciding whether to believe me. "I'm sorry, Zeke. I'm scared."

My heart thumps with annoyance. "Fuck, Azadeh, this is me. You think I'd do something to piss you off like this?"

Azadeh nods and walks toward Lev. My shoulders relax. Maybe all this will blow over. Azadeh and Lev have always had a fucked-up love-hate relationship. They have a lot of love for each other but can't seem to express it in a healthy way. It makes sense as neither had peaceful early years.

"Where is she, Lev?" Azadeh's voice is cold. It's the crazy calm tone that tells me I might find

Lev's head rolling by my feet if she doesn't get what she wants.

Lev glares down at her. "You ready to meet my demands?"

"No, Lev, I'm not. After this, you'll never see me again. I'm taking my sister and getting as far away from your psychotic ass as I can."

Lev nods. "It's unfortunate we couldn't reach an agreement, and neither of us will get what we want."

Azadeh's hand moves to her belt, and she unsheathes a sharp knife. Before she does something she'll regret, I grab her waist and haul her toward me. I'm confident she won't stab me with it. Well, I hope she won't. My chances look a whole lot better than Lev's.

Her scream is shrill, and she kicks out, narrowly missing my dick.

I sink my teeth into her shoulder to calm her the fuck down. "You know that's a valuable appendage, right? I can live with one eye, but if you fuck my dick up, I'm not sure I'll survive."

Azadeh ignores my joke as she thrashes in my arms, pushing and shoving to wiggle free. "I'm gonna kill you, Lev. I'm going to stand over your body and laugh as I fucking slice and dice each of your organs until all that's left is gutted flesh and bones."

Fuck. She's seething. I've never seen her like this. Azadeh leans forward, and the next thing I know, a wad of spit hits the corner of Lev's mouth.

Lev's gaze moves from me to Azadeh. Without a word, he lifts his index finger to the spit and slides it into his mouth. "You shouldn't have stayed away this long."

"Anyone want to tell me what the fuck is going on?" I demand.

Azadeh turns her head, eyes bloodshot and wild. "Why don't you ask him?"

Chapter 4

Lev   Age 22
Hospital

I watched as Azadeh held her mother's hand, trying to stay strong for everyone while pushing back her own fears. Her brother Dariyus was pacing, voice raised, speaking rapidly in Persian. I assumed from the reaction of their youngest sister, Mona, that his words were more in line with the vile nature of the language. Even while drowning in the depths of sorrow, Azadeh still held the radiance of the sun.

She rose from beside her mother's bed as the nurse came in to administer medication not designed for healing but for comfort. My heart broke for my Beauty, another loss for a girl who'd already lost so much. I watched as she said something to her brother and turned to the door.

When Azadeh spotted me, she offered a shy wave and a small smile—a dim comparison to when she saw Cyrus or Zeke. My heart quickened with every step she took toward me, and I was reminded of how much power this girl held over me.

Usually, I wouldn't be caught dead in a hospital. My earliest memories of the institutions were muddled with blood, loss, and devastation. But I'd overheard Azadeh speaking to Zeke about how the hospital would be filled with family and friends stopping by to lend a hand and provide an ear if they were in Iran. Her voice broke when she spoke about the sense of community in Iran she would never hope to find here. I knew that friends were a source of support in times of sadness and joy in Azadeh's culture. Since her family didn't have those bonds in America, I wanted to be that support, even in a small way.

"Thank you for coming, Lev," she whispered.

I nodded, swallowing the tightness in my throat, unable to form words. Talking wasn't my forte, but my brain forgot how to vocalize when it came to Azadeh.

Azadeh's face scrunched as if she were pondering how to salvage an uncomfortable situation. I wanted to kick my ass for being so awkward around her. How hard would it be to simply say, "I'm sorry about your mom, Azadeh."

"Az!" Cyrus and Zeke shouted in unison as they barreled out of the elevator to where Azadeh and I were standing.

Zeke rushed to her and wrapped his arms around her. Azadeh placed her head on his shoulder, trembling as she fisted the back of his hoodie. Another pang of jealousy festered in my soul at how easy it was for Zeke to comfort her.

Zeke rubbed her back and cooed in her ear, "It's okay, Princess. It's all gonna be okay."

"They've gotta be able to do something, right?" Cyrus demanded, fidgeting with the platinum zippo in his hand.

"Are you fuckin' crazy playing with that here?" I growled.

Cyrus eyed the hospital staff to see if anyone was watching his stupidity. He glared at me for a moment before the left side of his lips curled up in one of those idiotically charming smiles. "Don't worry. I'm not suicidal," he said as he flipped the zippo open and closed. "I won't ignite it. Wouldn't want us to blow up or anything."

Azadeh laughed at Cyrus, and a hundred-pound weight lifted off my chest. I was happy he'd put a smile on her face, but I couldn't help wishing it was me who'd done it.

Zeke kept his arm around her shoulders and tucked her against him protectively. "How's your maman?"

Azadeh inhaled a shaky breath as if desperate to hold her tears at bay. "She's dying, Ezekiel. She's dying, and there's nothing I can do. I can't even afford to get her a private room away from the loud woman. Her insurance only covered semi-private, and when we checked, the prices of a private room started at ten thousand a night. Dariyus says he can get the money, but I have no idea what he'd have to do to get it, and I don't want my mother's last thoughts of her son to be disappointment."

Azadeh buried her face in her hands and gently sobbed. The only emotion her sorrow forced out of me was irrational anger. I was tired of life constantly dealing blow after blow to the people I cared about and my ingrained inability to express sympathy or any attempt at comfort. I couldn't stand by and listen to her wail when I was too helpless and pathetic to do anything for her.

So I walked away.

Chapter 5

Lev   Age 30
Present Day

The sting from Azadeh's hand lingers on my cheek. I suppose I should be glad it wasn't her right hook. Azadeh punches like a heavy-weight boxer.

Her chest heaves, and her eyes blaze fury at me. I'll need to sleep with one eye open tonight. The fury is nothing new. Azadeh has never looked at me with softness, even when I stepped up and did right by her. But it's okay because I don't need her to love me as long as I have her near me.

If only she'd come home one month earlier. But instead of coming here between jobs like she has for the last ten years, she decided to take up residency with the Cinders—three brothers known for barbaric cruelty and ruthlessness.

She'd rather take a job with them than come home and be with us.

I'd had to free her from the grip of Alaric and his two psycho brothers. My methods may not have been tasteful, but my reasons were sound.

I adjust the knot of my tie, suddenly feeling like it's strangling me. "You hungry, Azadeh? I don't know if they have anything of true sustenance at that debauchery club where you work."

Azadeh glares at me. "I always knew you were a little fucked, Lev, but now I have confirmation that you're a fucking psychopath."

If those words were spoken by a stranger, they wouldn't garner a reaction because they would be meaningless. But those taunting words coming from Azadeh's mouth—words from my past uttered to grind me into dust—are like a serrated blade cutting into my flesh. For the first time in my life, her words wound. "Since you believe me to be a psycho, Azadeh, and you're well aware of what I'm capable of, perhaps you should refrain from poking the bear."

Azadeh bares her teeth, her lips curling as she tugs against Zeke's tight hold. After a moment of fruitless struggling, she latches onto Zeke's arm with her mouth.

"Fuck!" Zeke yells, abandoning his hold on her waist. "You fuckin' bit me. Jesus, Az! What the hell has gotten into you?"

Azadeh's eyes flicker as she notices the trickle of blood gliding down Zeke's forearm, and her anger dissipates.

She gently takes his arm, remorse evident on her elegant face. Her teeth are no longer bared. Her eyes are back to their soft brown, and her fingers trail his flesh with tenderness. "Zeke, I'm so sorry."

A pang of jealousy churns in my heart like a tornado poised to destroy everything in its path. A part of me longs for her gentle touch, to experience the sensations the brush of her fingertips gliding along my skin would evoke.

But you won't let her.

The pesky voice whispers in the back of my mind, reminding me that the current status of my relationship with Azadeh is my fault.

Shoving my intrusive thoughts away, I pack them tightly in the many compartments I've forged in my fragile mind. I push through with the long-held steadfast resolve that all my shortcomings shouldn't matter, at least not for her. Azadeh always sees past everyone's monsters, ready to put her fears aside to discover the shred of goodness buried deep in a person's soul. But she's always been too frightened to sit with my demons. All she's ever offered me is civil tolerance.

"Hellcat," Cyrus says as he rushes toward Azadeh. He stops dead in his tracks when he sees her dark scowl. "Okay, this isn't a happy visit. You mad at us, Kitten? Is that why you've stayed away all this time?"

"It depends. Did you help Lev?"

"Help him with what? I keep trying to unload that stick out of his ass, but he seems to be very fond of it." Cyrus chuckles arrogantly and points in my direction. "I mean, look at the fucker. He's hanging around the house on a Monday morning dressed like he's going to a wedding at Buckingham Palace."

I scoff at his remark. "We can't all mimic the dress code of a junkie on skid row."

Cyrus glances at his ripped black jeans, combat boots and smiley face Nirvana t-shirt before dragging his eyes to me. "Doesn't matter what you think. Chicks dig the fit, bro." He wags his eyebrows. "Don't forget, I'm the one who bagged Azadeh, and your dick is about to get a disease from the blue balls you're packin'."

I want to lash out like a spoiled child at Cyrus's dig. He's pouring salt and citrus on a wound that'll never heal. But it's true we haven't been able to get all of her, no matter how much Zeke and Cyrus talk about her multiple orgasms in one night. Had they been able to "dickmatize" her, as they say, to stay with us, my actions wouldn't have been necessary.

"Your performance last time must not have been adequate, Cyrus. I've heard that when some men hit thirty, their libido takes a dive, and they require assistance. I'd be happy to get my physician to write a prescription for you if you think that would help."

Cyrus's jaw ticks as his hand glides into his jeans pocket, and he produces his silver zippo. His smile widens like a predator spotting its prey, and he bares his teeth.

In a flash, the wick of the zippo ignites, and Cyrus pounces on me. He grabs my tie, pulling at it until the tip is on fire. "It's been a minute since I've witnessed someone burn. I miss the stench of charred flesh."

I don't move as I watch the flame creeping up my tie, almost relishing the image Cyrus paints.

"You're fuckin' crazy!" Azadeh shouts.

She sounds like an angel. I'm okay with a miserable demise if it's her sweet voice carrying me to the devil. There are worse ways to perish.

Azadeh leaps on Cyrus and pulls him off. I roll on the ground to extinguish the flames eating toward my face. She saved my life. After what I did, she still couldn't bear to see me suffer. Perhaps she does harbor tender feelings for me, even when she adamantly denies their existence.

"Can the two of you tell me what's going on?" Zeke demands in a frustrated tone. "Y'all are out here acting crazier than usual."

I rise from the floor and dust the burned threads from my tie before digging into my pocket and pulling out my phone. I open up my email and point the screen toward Zeke.

"They've got Mona. I thought she was secure in the basement, but apparently, she's a little like her sister and had a few tricks up her sleeve. She escaped, and the wrong man has her captive."

"She escaped?" Zeke echoes, dumbfounded. "You had Mona? Here? How the fuck did you keep her a secret without either of us knowing?"

I stare at Zeke blankly. "It's easy to hide when no one sees you."

Chapter 6

Azadeh   Age 22
The Hospital

It wasn't a slap to my face when Lev walked away at the hospital. It was a fucking bulldozer to my gut. I never understood why Lev wanted the three of us around when he never seemed to be present. It wasn't only in times of sorrow; I understood not wanting to be around sadness. Some people couldn't process in a way that made them feel helpful. But Lev wasn't only distant in those moments. He was also absent in times of genuine joy. His mind roamed to a faraway place, and all we had was the shell of his physical form. Occasionally, I sensed he hated being in our presence, but the messed-up trauma bond he had with Zeke and Cyrus kept him by our sides.

"What do you need?" Zeke asked, shaking me from my thoughts of Lev.

I smiled at Zeke. His arms had offered comfort and strength for as long as I'd known him. He made things easier for me, and being around him made me feel cherished and safe. Zeke was a blessing in my life, a gift given to me for all the bad things I'd gone through. "You being here is enough."

Zeke had always been my refuge, someone I could turn to, knowing he'd be on my side no matter what. I was confident I could do nothing to make this man turn away from me. Even as a boy, he was my constant, no matter that his loyalty and fiercely protective nature had lost him something of great value.

I smiled as I thought about how Zeke was the epitome of a noble warrior or king in those old Persian tales in the pages of the Shahnameh. Valiant, resilient, passionate, and brave. He was the perfect prince riding to my rescue, but as much as I wanted to stand behind him and let him protect me, my past wouldn't allow it. Sometimes, I wished I could blindly lean on him because I knew this man would make me the happiest person on earth. Zeke would take care of me, and I'd never want for anything—traits that made me love him deeply and passionately. Zeke made my world lighter.

Trying to be strong for Dariyus and Mona was exhausting. Dar was so angry. He wanted to ask his friend Ezra for money, but I wouldn't let him. Ezra was a good guy, but he was affiliated with some scary people. I didn't want my mother's heart to break right before she died.

And then there was Mona. I thought she was scared more than anything else. Eighteen and an orphan. We didn't have any extended family here. No aunts or uncles. In Iran, losing a loved one brought family and the community together in a show of support.

"Some days, I feel like life has been one giant hurdle after another for my family. I don't know how to stop. It's like we're cursed."

Zeke placed a chaste kiss on my head and whispered, "There's no such thing as curses. Life is circumstance and luck. Everything we go through is a crapshoot. Gambling is supposed to be bad for us, but our lives are a game of chance from the moment of conception."

"I believe that. Life is a long game of craps. In the blink of an eye, I could've been one of the innocent girls in Evin Prison. It could've been worse in that situation. Dar and Mona would've been alone, with no one to look out for them."

I looked at Zeke, admiring the structure of his handsome face, which was even more attractive with his black eye patch. His gaze was focused on Maman's room. She looked like a peaceful angel, thanks to the drugs. My brother sat by her bed, elbows on his knees, while Mona was curled in a ball beside him.

I sighed wearily. "She was so angry when I chose to study martial arts in Japan instead of going to school and becoming a doctor. She told me I was ruining my life and spitting on all the sacrifices she'd made for me. She was right, you know. Not about the martial arts. But about me spitting on her sacrifices."

Zeke turned me to face him, gripping my shoulders. "Az, that woman loved you. She left everything she knew, traveled to the other side of the world, sacrificed everything familiar, and worked herself to the bone so that her kids could live. What would make your mother proud is for you to keep doing exactly what you've been doing. She's raised such a beautiful, strong, independent, and loving human, Az. I think the reason she said what she said wasn't because she was disappointed in you. It was because she was scared."

Zeke was a bridge. He never tried to keep me from soaring. Never tried to hold me down or in place. Since we were kids, Zeke had bent until he broke so I could walk an easier road without fear of falling.

I tilted my head and gazed up at Zeke. He looked like he had a halo under the fluorescent hospital lights, which was fitting because he'd been my guardian angel for years. "What would she be scared of here?"

Zeke smiled and sighed, the type of sigh a parent might give their child when they purposely misunderstood their point. Usually, that would've gotten Zeke a knee to his balls, but I was too miserable to be insulted. "She escaped Iran with her three kids so they would be safe, and you work in remote parts of the world rescuing girls from the same kind of men she ran from."

Tears poured from my eyes as my brain soaked up every syllable like a sponge, and Zeke's words sank in. I'd helped a lot of women over the last few years, but the one person I desperately wanted to rescue was the only person I was bound to let down.

My mother had saved my life, but I couldn't save hers.

"Got you some hot chocolate," Cyrus said, holding out a white and yellow Styrofoam cup with a plastic lid.

I'd been so lost in conversation with Zeke that I hadn't noticed Cyrus had left, which seemed impossible because everyone was always aware of Cyrus.

"It doesn't have whipped cream. What kind of beverage place doesn't stock whipped cream?" he demanded, outraged.

"A hospital that doesn't concern itself with fancy drinks and Instagram-worthy photo opportunities," Lev's deep baritone answered behind me, making me jolt and causing the hot liquid to bounce out of the cup onto my hand.

I opened my mouth to scold him about sneaking up on people when I saw two nurses and an orderly enter my mother's room.

"Excuse me, what's happening?" I asked, marching back to the room.

One of the nurses smiled. "Your mother is being moved to the executive floor."

My heart accelerated. The last thing we needed was a bill for tens of thousands of dollars for my mother to sleep in a fancy hospital room. I knew the hospital wouldn't care that it was their error; they'd push and pull until they could squeeze something out of my family. "There must be a mistake. We don't have that kind of money."

"It's already been paid for in full, Miss Baran."

"Who would possibly pay for this?" I demanded.

"Whoever it was is a very good friend, it seems."

No one I knew had that kind of money. No one, except... I turned to the guys waiting in the hallway, and my gaze zeroed in on the moody man in a hoodie.

Levinston Cartwright.

Chapter 7

Azadeh   Age 29
Present Day

Conflicted emotions burn within me, ranging from homicidal rage to sympathy and compassion. I despise every single one of them except rage. I hold on to anger and let it consume me until it flares brightly in my mind and heart.

My gaze moves to Lev's face. I note the dullness in his gray eyes and his stiff stature. Unlike Cyrus and Zeke, Lev's never been able to relax fully. That's probably why he's assumed an image beyond reproach. Prim and proper, the perfect facade for a man who wants to keep his darkest secrets hidden from prying eyes. Lev has always presented as hard and cold, but underneath, he has moments of altruism.

I squash down any fondness lingering in my heart for Lev. He deserves an ass-kicking for what he's done. I still think this is a nightmare I'm about to wake up from. "Is that why you took my sister, Lev? Because you weren't getting enough attention? Ever thought about seeing a professional for that? Therapy works wonders. Trust me, I did it for years."

Lev steps forward, using his immense height as a fucked-up intimidation tactic as he towers over me. I reach behind me, grabbing Cyrus's shirt and tugging him forward.

"What's happening here? You wanna get naked?" Cyrus asks, lifting the hem of his shirt.

Fuck a guy a few times, and he thinks any touch means he's about to get his dick wet.

"Bend over," I demand. "I need a lift."

Cyrus obediently crouches on the ground and grabs my ankles, hoisting me onto his shoulders.

"Step closer to Lev."

Cyrus chuckles and gets right in Lev's face.

I gaze down at Lev and smirk. "What was it you were saying, Lev?"

Lev's eyes narrow. "You're acting childish."

I don't care how childish I'm being. Don't give two fucks. He's lucky all I'm being is childish and not stabbing him in the eye repeatedly for losing my sister after his pompous ass kidnapped her. "I want my sister, Lev. You better know where she is and have a plan to get her back, or you'll be sleeping with one eye open for the rest of your life."

"I know where she is. We just need to go in and get her," Lev says, walking away.

I twist my fingers in Cyrus's hair and tug him forward. He follows Lev to the dining room table as if he knows exactly what to do. Usually, it gets on my nerves how much Cyrus enjoys pushing Lev's buttons, but I'm thoroughly enjoying it right now.

On the white porcelain table are blueprints and various other papers.

"What's all this?" I ask, smacking Cyrus on the shoulder.

Cy grabs my waist, lifts me off his shoulders, and places me on my feet in one smooth movement.

Lev glides his hand over the table. "These are things we need to know to break into the compound and rescue Mona."

I glare at him. "We wouldn't need any of this had your idiot self not taken her."

"You should've come back. It was inconvenient for me. I had too much on my plate to check in."

I narrow my eyes on him. "What do you mean, too much on your plate to check in on me?"

Lev appears nervous. He quickly averts his eyes, focusing on the various blueprints on the table.

"What did you mean, Lev?"

"Just fuckin' tell her," Cyrus demands, rolling his eyes.

I know there's more to this story, but staying on track to find my sister is far more important than any other idiotic thing Lev may or may not have done.

Lev adjusts his tie. "There's nothing to tell. Now, how about we stop wasting time and continue our plans to get Mona back?"

Chapter 8

Lev   Age 25

Dublin. Ireland

Love made me pathetic, and obsession made me insane—both sentiments bestowed upon me from the moment I laid eyes on Azadeh Baran. Until Azadeh, I didn't believe goodness existed in the world. My whole life had been an extensive exercise on how to manipulate, use, and discard people for pleasure. I was surrounded by monsters pretending to be otherwise in society's prying eyes.

Then Azadeh came into my life, and I discovered that kindness and compassion were tangible virtues. But with that newfound knowledge of goodness, an over-whelming need to consume bloomed. That desperation led me to become a shadow who lurked in the darkness to be near Azadeh, whether or not she wished for it.

Cyrus, Zeke, and I were released from the institution at nineteen. Azadeh had been there for us the whole *time. Originally, she was Zeke's, but during our two years together, she belonged to all of us in one way or another. When it came to Azadeh, we were loyal soldiers ready to lay down our lives if she demanded it. I was prepared to be her sword and attack anyone I perceived as a threat to my angel.*

After her mother's passing, Azadeh's visits home became more seldom. She drowned herself in her work, gallivanting all over the world as a vigilante to save other women from dangerous and precarious situations.

I could've been more like Zeke, confident in my abilities, but Zeke didn't need her to breathe like I did. She didn't consume his thoughts, actions, and motives like she did mine. Unlike Ezekiel, I couldn't sit idly at home, keeping the fire burning for random visits from our girl. I craved her, and if I went too long without seeing her, it ripped my world apart like a piece of meat between the jaws of ravenous wolves.

That was how I found myself in the alley of a run-down bar in Dublin across from Azadeh's apartment, glaring at a man who'd tried to kiss her.

When he leaned in, his arm above her head, I was ready to rip his spine out of his back. But then Azadeh pushed him off and closed the door.

The man appeared irritated, but nothing to cause a significant alarm. Then the fucker gazed up at her window and walked around the back, trying the handle of the side door.

He didn't see me coming. Being the child of monsters, I'd learned to shield any sound and move like air.

"You need help?" I asked.

"Hey, man," he said, looking rattled as he pushed a hand through his greasy blond hair. "Yeah, my bitch is mad at me. Locked me out." He smirked when I didn't respond. "You know how these bitches are."

I stepped closer, enough to demonstrate the difference in our height. The man was no taller than five-ten. Judging by his rapid retreat, he was intimidated by my six-four frame.

"No, I don't know how these bitches are," I spat, keeping my voice cool and level. One thing I'd learned about distasteful men was that a level voice and a calm demeanor unnerved them more than aggression ever could.

The guy stammered, flailing his arms like a marionette, unsure of his next move. He stepped back again, desperate to put some space between us. I closed the distance until the backs of his legs hit a metal garbage can. He jostled it, and the lid hit the cement with a loud clang.

"You know, man," he cajoled. "Those bitches who ask for it, and as soon as things heat up, they pretend like they don't want it. You should've seen what the slut was wearing. Tight leather pants and a midriff top showing skin and cut so low, her tits were almost hanging out. She had no problem letting me buy her drinks earlier. Took my money like they all do. Fuckin' whores. But when it was time to put out, she was like a fuckin' meat locker. Ice cold."

He held up his hand, showing me his slightly crooked finger. "This one even took out my finger. Can you believe that? I was only trying to have a good time, and she fucking attacked me. Now the bitch gotta pay. I got a reputation to keep. Can't have anyone finding out about what that bitch did to me without knowing how I made her pay."

Without thinking, I pulled out my colt and shot him in the leg. The fucker stumbled, howling in pain as he grabbed his knee. That finally shut him up. Fucker was in so much pain that the only thing he could do was gasp air into his worthless lungs.

"This gun is one of a pair carved from a five-million-year-old meteorite. The other one in the set is with

that girl you disrespected." I tipped my head toward the house as I stepped closer.

The guy scooted back on his elbows, wide eyes silently pleading as he looked up at me in horror.

The asshole thought I'd waste a second of sympathy or remorse on him.

"Please. I'll go home and forget about everything. Bro, I need a doctor. I think that bullet is lodged in my knee," he pleaded between pained gasps.

I bent and smirked at him. The scum screeched into the night as I dug my fingers into the wound, probing until I gripped the bullet and pulled it out. I stabbed the new hole I'd made with the barrel of my gun a few times for good measure.

Rising, I held the silver bullet to his face. "This won't bother you any longer."

The vermin's eyes widened as he attempted to push himself off the dirty cement.

I lifted my foot and slammed it against his chest, forcing him back down. "Not so fast."

"What do you want from me?" he whispered.

I kneeled and shoved the barrel of the gun against his face. "You tried to harm someone who belongs to me, and you also made a mess of my gun. I think it's only right that you clean it up."

The man wiggled and shook his head as I pushed the blood-covered barrel between his lips until the whole thing was in his mouth. "Now, be a good boy and clean it. Make sure you suck off all your blood."

He shook his head again, and I cocked the gun. "Clean it. Suck it like you're sucking cock. Better make a show of it, or I might get upset and accidentally unload a bullet in your worthless mouth."

The motherfucker moved his mouth up and down on the barrel like an enthusiastic call girl impressing her best client. He gagged, and his eyes watered.

A perverse sense of satisfaction came over me as I witnessed his expert blow job abilities. "Atta boy."

His eyes found mine as I pulled the trigger, splattering the wall and my suit with his worthless brains.

Chapter 9

Cyrus — Age 30
Present Day

We've been sitting at the table for hours, listening to Lev's plans.

Apparently, the fucker took Mona from her school and locked her up downstairs for weeks. I do some out-of-pocket shit, but I don't fuck with my own. Well, unless they want some, then I deliver every single time. I sure as fuck wouldn't do anything to Mona. She's family. You don't fuck with family. Unless it's your biological one who created your mentally unbalanced personality. Those fuckers you let burn in your childhood home as you watch with glee from the front yard. The same yard they forced you to take the yearly perfect nuclear family photos they sent to friends and clients.

My legs bounce up and down, and irritation creeps in. I don't know if I need a smoke or if I have the urge to watch something light the fuck up. "I'm all for takin' out some motherfuckers, but even I think this is some fucked up shit, Lev."

Lev grabs his charred tie and removes it. He's probably ensuring no one tries to strangle him with it or set him on fire again. I'm shocked that Azadeh hasn't already stabbed him to death. I lean back and stare at her with a smile. *She loves us.*

"Why are you smiling like a psycho?" Azadeh asks.

She's so cute when she's annoyed with me. Who am I kidding? She's always cute. I like how her right eyebrow arches when I do something stupid. She wags her fingers and tells me I'm an idiot.

"I was thinking about how hot it's gonna be watching you slit some throats. We should bang on that. Not so much into the whole blood scene, but I'd walk on the wild side for you, Hellcat."

Azadeh shakes her head. "You're an idiot."

I place my hands behind my head and lean back in my chair. "I love you too, boo."

She keeps shaking her head, but I see the smile cracking her anger and her eyebrow lowering. "You're the only moron who takes an insult as a term of endearment."

"Nah, Hellcat. If you didn't insult me, I'd be worried."

"She's never insulted me," Lev says.

Sometimes, Lev makes it too easy to rile him up. "Last I checked, Levinston, you're the only one Hellcat hasn't fucked. And that was before you fucked up and lost her sister, so yeah, I'd say you should be worried. You should pray you'll wake up tomorrow morning."

Lev glares at me and growls—a full-blown big bear growl. I try to hold back my laughter but fail miserably. Fuck it, that shit is so funny.

Lev moves toward me, but Azadeh steps between us. "You two can have your pissing contest after we find my sister, okay?"

Lev nods and moves some sheets of paper on the table.

Unlike Lev, I've never been good at doing as I'm told. "We wouldn't be looking for Mona if Lev hadn't taken her."

Lev growls again in some sort of barbaric warning. I guess chicks are supposed to dig that shit, but it's annoying as fuck. What dude walks around growling like a wolf or a bear, some dumb forest animal? I blame those romance novels Azadeh reads. Lev probably reads them too. He's been stalking her since she came into our lives. I'm pretty sure those three-piece suits are for her benefit. That's how all these dudes dress. Big-ass mafia dons who look like Henry Cavill kidnap these women, and every chick has Stockholm Syndrome. He does some "Me Tarzan, you Jane" shit, and boom bam, the chick creams her pants for her captor to plow her. So the chick thinks, yes, that's hot. My pussy is fucking wet. Like a faucet, baby.

I glance up and notice Az tracking Lev's movements. Holy shit, her pupils are dilating. Is she breathing heavier? Well fuck, that's annoying.

Azadeh places her hands on Lev's chest. He flinches, and she drops her arms. Shit, the man's an idiot. I've been as hard as granite from the moment I saw her. If she touched any part of my body, I'd have her bent over with my cock deep in any of her decadent holes. Had Lev not been a fuckin' moron and taken her sister, that's what I'd be doing this minute. Then again, she might not have shown up had Lev not done the fucked-up shit he did.

I mentally bat away the intrusive thoughts supporting Lev's actions. Had he taken her and kept her safe, none of this would be a big deal. Az would've yelled, and I would've made it up to her by letting her ride my face until she came all over it.

I don't know what it is about Az, but she's the only girl who's ever got my motor going. No other girl's been able to do that. I thought I only liked dick, but Azadeh got a hold of my fuckin' heart and squeezed it so damn tight. Every day, my heart expands for this girl. She's so easy to love, which is why she's had us in her pocket for fifteen years.

Chapter 10

Cyrus   Age 20
Cyrus and Zeke's Apartment

"**Y**ou picture her when you fuck me?" I asked Zeke as he panted beneath me.

"No," he moans. "I guess it started that way, but I've discovered feelings are fluid."

I clamped his earlobe between my teeth and tugged gently, appreciating his honest answer. My feelings for Azadeh weren't like Zeke's when I first met her. I saw her as competition for his affection, but as I got to know her, I yearned for her too. The girl had a way of twisting you up until the only thing you wanted in life was to pledge your undying loyalty to her. That whole notion was a fuckin' hard pill for me to swallow as I didn't believe in monogamy, but between her and Zeke, I was so fulfilled and didn't need anything or anyone else. They both loved Lev, so I had to deal *with that fucker. I had to admit he was fuckin' hot in a stuck-up asshole kind of way.*

"How are you holding up?" I asked as I poured the isopropyl in small streaks down his broad back.

Zeke chuckled. "If someone asked me five years ago if I'd let one of my best friends light me up before he fucked me, I would've laughed in their face. But fuck, this shit is all kinds of relaxing. It almost deludes me into thinking I could take that giant ass cock of yours with no lube."

I smiled as I grabbed the torch, streaking a flame along Zeke's taut muscles before putting it out. I had a sick and twisted impulse to allow the flames to penetrate his skin and sear his flesh, releasing the stench of burning tissue. I pushed back my baser impulses and forced myself to remain in the realm of sanity, putting Zeke's safety above my depraved and twisted desires.

Zeke had no issue remaining still beneath me. I think he liked the beauty of motionlessness, but I always tied him down to be safe. He was face down, arms raised over his head, tied with rope, and I spread his legs, tying them to the footboard. He asked me once why I didn't use the spreader bar and handcuffs. I looked him directly in the eye and explained that cutting him out of fabric was easier than metal. It shocked me that he still agreed to be restrained after hearing that. I was glad he trusted me. Not many people would. After all, I was the crazy kid who burned his parents to a crisp.

I bounced the torch along Zeke's skin until I landed between his thighs. Zeke's cock thrust from his groin as hard as steel. I licked my lips, thinking how fuckin' hot it would be to see fire, even for a moment, on the tip. Bending, I licked his precum, relishing his salty flavor.

I put out the fire and placed the torch on its stand, turning back to the hot-as-fuck man lying ass up on my bed. "I want to fuck you," I groaned, kneeling behind him.

"I want to be fucked," Zeke responded.

I grabbed his tight ass, pulling his cheeks apart to expose his puckered asshole, and spat. Zeke raised his ass, letting me know he wanted me to tear into him and fuck him until he passed the fuck out.

Using my spit, I pushed the tip of my finger in, relishing his moan. Closing my eyes, I fought my violent desires. I always had to push those desires down as far as I could. I was fucked up to want to harm someone I loved, but I'd never had lessons in healthy relationships. The only things I knew were brutality and violence. Until I met Azadeh and Zeke, I had no idea about the magical ability of a gentle touch.

I reached for the lube and poured it on my fingers, letting some drip down his crack before massaging it into his ass. I pushed a finger inside him to the knuckle before adding a second, then a third. "I'm going to fuck you raw, Zeke."

"Stop talking about what you're going to do to me and do it."

I pulled my fingers out of him and lined up my cock. With one thrust, I was sheathed in his tight asshole. "You feel so good, baby boy. So fuckin' good. How does it feel knowing I'm going to unload all my cum and watch it leak out of your tight ass?"

"Fuck," Zeke said through clenched teeth. "You're so fuckin' big."

I thrust into him. "You're being"—thrust—"such a good"—thrust—"little"—thrust—"ass whore."

Zeke groaned as I continued to pound into his asshole mercilessly.

I twisted my fingers in his thick hair and yanked his head back, forcing him to look up at me. I used my other hand to pry his full lips open, shoving four fingers into his mouth and relishing his gagging noises. "That's it, baby boy. Gag for me. I want both of your holes filled with me."

Zeke tugged at his restraints, his dominant nature fighting to take over. Restraints weren't my thing. I used them for fire play, but fuckin someone all tied up didn't rev my engines. Yet watching Zeke struggle underneath me was as hot as fuck.

I removed my hand from his mouth, and his drool landed on the bed. I smiled before crushing my lips to his.

"Well, what do we have here?"

I turned my head to see Azadeh standing by the door.

"Az," Zeke said as he tugged on the restraints.

"Please don't rush on my account. The show is... stimulating."

As much as having a hot girl watch me fuck was a turn-on, Zeke was too freaked the fuck out for me to enjoy it. It wasn't like Azadeh didn't know we fucked. She even joined in on the fun. That was her thing, dropping by every month or two, blowing our minds with rough sex, then jet-setting again. She was the only girl I knew who had three men wanting her but wasn't willing to settle the fuck down.

Zeke thrashed against his restraints like a fuckin' wild animal clamoring to escape his cage. I enjoyed control during sex, but this kind of shit freaked me out. I'd never worked out my hang-up. I was fine being dominated and having the shit fucked out of me. The bruises, marks, and body aches felt good, but I liked being the prey.

I didn't stop fucking Zeke even as he bucked beneath me. I was disgusted by my actions, but I had a perverse, twisted need to empty my balls deep in his ass.

A smirk formed on my lips as I stared at Azadeh. "I ain't rushing, Az. I'm going to fill our boy's ass, and then I'll be with you."

Azadeh's eyes were hooded as we stared at each other. Her breathing matched the speed of my thrusts. She was my fucking metronome, keeping rhythm as I slaughtered Zeke's ass until I stiffened and came deep inside him.

I didn't linger long to enjoy the bliss of the afterglow. I jumped off Zeke and searched the room, desperate to find my knife. Fuckin' pretty irresponsible of me not to know exactly where it was. I would've been able to find it much easier if Azadeh wasn't staring at me with a mixture of lust, intrigue, and amusement.

I turned my head at Azadeh's soft giggle and glared at her.

She smiled and pulled my knife from her back pocket. "This might help."

I went to grab it, but she pulled her arm back. She might not have been in the institution with us, but the girl sure had a few screws loose. Her teeth slid along her bottom lip, and her pretty pink tongue poked out as if offering a challenge,

"Sweetheart, you gonna give me that blade, or are we gonna stand here gawking at each other all night?"

Azadeh stepped closer. Without a word, she traced the jagged burn marks on my face with the tip of the blade, etching her way over the dips and curves as if painting a little picture in her brain. I fuckin' hated how most people stared at my face. Their eyes brimmed with pity, sadness, and fear. But not Azadeh. She regarded me with intrigue and lust.

"Scars are maps. They show the roads taken on a journey. I think yours are interesting."

I always wondered what Azadeh knew about scars. Sure, she'd gained scars during her immigration journey, but her family was great. Her brother was a pretty cool dude, and she had the most adorable kid sister who worshiped her. Her mother was a fuckin' saint. Az said her mother was overbearing, but I saw it as a parent's fierce protective love for their child. It made sense to be a little over the top for those you cared about. At least her mom gave too many shits. Mine didn't give one.

Aside from her amazing family, she was also beautiful. Stunning. She was so fuckin' radiant. When the girl walked into the room, we lesser mortals paused to watch her. Long, black hair that fell in pretty curls to her sexy-as-fuck ass. Big almond-shaped eyes. As weird as it was for me to notice, the girl had naturally thick, long lashes that mascara companies could only dream about. Her lips were full, and her body... God, her body! Curves for days. Great tits, nice big ass I wanted to bite, and thick thighs that would look good wrapped around my neck, suffocating me as I ate to my heart's content.

I grabbed her wrist, and we stared at each other. Fuck, those eyes were something else. Deep pools a man could drown in. "What would you know about scars, sweetheart?"

She tugged at her arm and smiled when I wouldn't release it. "Gotta let go so I can show you."

Reluctantly, I deprived myself of her touch. But fuck, that pain was immediately extinguished as she used the tip of the blade to lift the hem of her black tank top, pulling it up over her sexy-as-fuck double D tits covered in black lace. She never took off her shirt when we fucked. I'd tried to remove it once, and she'd pulled her knife and held it to my wrist, telling me if I didn't stop, I'd need a hook to replace my fingers.

My cock was fuckin' straining like a soldier in a damn military parade. "Still not seeing any scars, baby. All I see is mountains whose peaks I want to touch."

She laughed and turned.

My. Fucking. God.

Her back. Her entire back was covered in a crisscross pattern of healed wounds.

Chapter 11

Zeke Age 29
Present Day

W hat are you supposed to do when you're in love with three people, and one of them betrays and harms the other? It's a frustrating and confusing situation.

Part of me sympathizes with Lev. The guy is pretty fucked up, and I can see how that wheel in his brain would think that kidnapping Mona would force Azadeh to come to the manor. But for Christ's sake, he should've known our girl would slice his dick off for messing with her kid sister.

Another part of me wants to fuckin' beat his head in until a pool of blood frames his pretty little face. Mona. The motherfucker took Mona. I glance between Lev and Azadeh, trying to gauge on a scale of one to ten how homicidal she is.

Azadeh's face is blank, which scares me more than her anger. She doesn't hide her emotions. When we were kids, her mother worried how the neighbors would judge her, but Azadeh didn't care. Her response to her mother was, "Did you bring me to America to worry about the chatter of pathetic gossip or so I could be free?" Her mother mumbled something under her breath and shook her head—Mrs. Baran's version of "I'll turn my head, and you do what you want, but if you get caught, I'll punish you." I discovered that way of thinking was common in Persian culture. Don't ask and don't tell—a whole damn cultural philosophy.

At first, I assumed it was a religious aspect, but the Barans had no fondness or affiliation with a god of any shape or form. I think that's what attracted me to the family. I loved being around Azadeh, but her mother became important to me. Nasrin Baran had many opinions but lacked a judgmental bone in her body. Being in their company allowed me a reprieve from my psychotic preacher father and robot mother.

My affinity with the Barans Is why I have the urge to snap Lev's neck and watch his dead body fall at my feet. I've never wanted to harm Lev before. If anything, I'm fiercely protective of him. What he's gone through is far worse in many ways than the trauma Cyrus and I are burdened with. The only negative emotion I've ever harbored toward Lev was jealousy, and I knew that was fucked up.

It's fucked up to be jealous of someone I love, and I love Lev deeply. So much that not being with him romantically is like a razor cutting through my soul. But Lev and Azadeh have a connection I'll never understand. Both of them were party to a systematic type of abuse that caused severe scars that hide below the surface. The world sees my and Cyrus's damage, but Azadeh and Lev's trauma isn't worn on their flesh. It's ingrained in their minds.

I touch the patch covering my eye, and my mind wanders to the night I lost it. When Azadeh, Nasrin, and Mona rushed me to the hospital after my father gouged out my eye with a soup spoon. They held my hand and told a shit-scared seventeen-year-old kid it would all be okay. Nasrin even told me I could live with them. She said she'd fight my parents. I knew that wasn't possible because she'd never be able to go toe to toe with my dad, the great Reverend Joseph Summers. I appreciated her sentiment since she was the first adult to give a damn about me. But no one believed my father beat the shit out of me, let alone that he was capable of strapping me down as he scooped my eyeball from my socket like a child digging for treasure in their ice cream cup.

My father took out his wrath on my flesh, some fucked up ritual to cast out his demons. Dearest Dad, who couldn't bear the world to unearth his greatest secret—his son's attraction to men. Guess finding gay porn under his pubescent son's mattress drove him to the edge. The man probably figured he'd beat my bisexuality out of me. God forbid his son got off on the idea of a cock up his ass while he pounded into a wet pussy.

That was the night Nasrin became more valuable than my mother, and the Barans became the family I would lay my life down for. It started with my falling in love with Azadeh and ended with Nasrin showing me what it was like to have the love of a true mother.

I killed my father after I got out of the hospital. Poetic justice, if you ask me. Took out the man's eyes with my mother's chef knife while I tied her to her mahogany dining room chair. That act got me two years in a psych ward, where I met Cyrus and Lev.

My mother's shrill screams during my first kill are still my soundtrack when violence is all I can see.

Chapter 12

Zeke Age 17

Azadeh's Modest Childhood Home

"God should never be forced, Ze-ek," Mrs. Baran said as she put ointment on my bruises and cuts. Her voice broke as she attempted to push back tears.

I should've bitten my tongue, but I was so full of emotional and physical pain that I wasn't willing to keep my thoughts in check. "The only feelings the mention of God conjures in me are dread, violence, and manipulation."

Mrs. Baran nodded.

It couldn't be easy to see the same marks on my body that scared her child. I didn't want to come here. All I wanted was Azadeh. After my father passed out, I climbed out my window and wobbled my way to her house. Usually, I would climb up to Azadeh's window *to avoid her mother, but my dad had mangled my leg a bit, so that wasn't a possibility. Instead, I threw rocks until Azadeh's head poked out. I guessed I should've checked out how messed up my face was before I headed over because she took one look at me and screamed, waking up everybody.*

Now, she offered a dry laugh at my thoughts about God. "That I can understand. When you force someone to eat, they're bound to get sick and throw up. With indoctrination, religious people sometimes have a gluttony problem."

Even through the pain, a smile formed on my lips when I heard Azadeh's voice. "So basically, my dad forced me into being bulimic?" Azadeh scanned my body as if searching for something that might not have been visible. "What are you hoping to find?"

She quickly averted her eyes like a kid caught with her hand in the cookie jar after her mother told her she couldn't have any more sweets. In those moments, I convinced myself Azadeh saw me as more than her best friend. Maybe she had deeper feelings for me.

I waited patiently for her answer. Even though Azadeh spoke English fluently now, sometimes she paused to search for the right word, so conversations needed my patience. But it didn't seem like a language barrier impeding her speech now. It was something more painful, something she'd rather forget.

I experienced a resounding need to push Azadeh for an answer. I despised seeing her sad. All I wanted was her smiles, and by coming to her to seek comfort, I'd opened a wound she yearned to keep sealed. Fuck. I'd kick my ass if my body wasn't pretty much useless.

"I'm sorry, Az. We don't need to talk about it."

Azadeh tilted her head and smiled. I loved how she had all these different smiles, and I knew every single one of them. This smile was one of reassurance. She had a sad smile, a happy one, a nervous one, a friendly one, a sweet one.

"There's nothing to be sorry about. I was just thinking about the irony."

"Irony?" I asked.

Azadeh was so cryptic. She used language in such a peculiar way. It was as if the conversation was in her mind, and she didn't see the need to articulate it with whoever was in her presence. She once joked about how Persian would sound like Yoda talking if translated word for word to English. I wondered if her mind was complex and intricate like that of the Master Jedi.

"I always thought the West would be this paradise where everyone was free to think, act, and say whatever they wanted. And to an extent, I suppose that's true. You don't have government officials arresting you because you said something about Jesus. No one will torture you if you don't follow the dress code. But I've come to realize that even here, some people are so desperate to get you to paradise that they force you to live in hell."

"Do you ever wonder if the world would be a better place if Abraham's mother had swallowed?" I regretted the words as soon as they left my mouth. Not the statement itself or that I might have insulted someone who so many believed was a prophet, but because they were so crass.

Everything about Azadeh was gentle. She wasn't a pushover or naïve, but she was gentle toward those she held close to her heart. She rarely swore, and she had a way of making you feel welcome. She would share her last morsel of food with a stranger because it was rude not to. I'd even seen her give away her sweater to a girl because she said it was lovely.

Later, Azadeh told me she loved that sweater, and when I asked her why she gave it away, she said it was custom. Apparently, Iranians had this thing called Tarof, but we Westerners had no clue that we weren't supposed to take what they were offering.

Tarof was the act of offering. I discovered through Nasrin that Tarof was this constant back-and-forth offering for someone to take and keep anything they complimented. I liked the custom. It made someone feel worthy. The only problem was that some people would take advantage of it.

"Sorry. Az. I should've watched my mouth."

Azadeh laughed. "Good old Abraham. I'm not sure if he was the problem or the four billion people who think God ordained a man with severe paranoid delusions and homicidal tendencies. Religion isn't evil, not by itself. If you take lessons from the texts, it could be a form of enrichment. It can help be a moral compass of sorts, but as soon as religion becomes an obsession, it morphs into poison, and that's when it becomes lethal to anyone who adheres to it. This is why so many people rage against it."

"Do you believe?" I asked.

"God? I'd like to think he or she is up there watching over us. I'd like to think whatever being God is, he's a good one, not one of vengeance or intolerance in organized religion. But to answer your question truthfully, wanting to

believe and believing are two vastly different things. No. I don't believe in God. Not anymore. I've seen what religion does to people. I don't want to live in the world of us and them. To place humans in neat little boxes where they're worthy or unworthy. Life doesn't work like that. And to be fair, the concept of free will and love thy neighbors that so many religions preach is stripped away until all empathy and humanity is tarnished."

I glanced at a framed black-and-white photo of a man and a woman with two young children by their side, a boy and a girl, no more than ten. They were standing under a monument in Tehran, The Azadi Tower. The woman was laughing, her hair blowing in the wind as the man looked on at her adoringly. "Who's that in the photo?"

"That's my grandparents with my mom and her twin brother. That was right before the revolution. They renamed it Azadi Tower. Can you believe that? The great freedom tower in Tehran symbolizes the opposite of freedom. Down with the monarchy only to replace it with a tyrannical theocracy. They killed thirty thousand people right after the revolution. Executed them in one go. Thirty-thousand people who didn't want a monarchy but didn't want to live under oppressive religious rule either. The killing didn't stop there. Anyone who dared to speak out against the regime was silenced with imprisonment, extortion,

blackmail, or death. The propaganda machine had people convinced Iranians wanted the current government, but they didn't. The revolution was stolen, swiped right from under those kids who had a dream of democracy." Azadeh shook her head as sadness welled up in her eyes. "What did all those young people fight for in the first place? The king didn't fall for freedom; he fell for a new form of oppression, far worse and far more lethal. Now, the country is mostly populated by people who never had a say but must now endure the foolish choices of their parents and grandparents with no hope of ending their suffering."

Mrs. Baran interrupted our deep conversation by handing me a hot cup of tea in a small clear mug with a lollipop stick standing at attention on the side.

"What's this?" I ask.

"This fixes everything," Mrs. Baran said with a warm smile. I found it a little jarring how she could be the sweetest mother on earth but also yell at her son like a damn drill sergeant. "Chai nabat."

"Translated to sweet tea, it's black tea with saffroninfused rock sugar," Azadeh said. Iranian mothers believe it will cure whatever ails you."

I took a sip and let the sweetness coat my throat. The liquid wasn't a medicine that could fix my abusive father or mend the aches he'd caused to my flesh. But the remedy given to me by the mother of the person I cared for more than anyone else in the world did wonders for my soul.

"You should rest, Ze-ek," Mrs. Baran said. "Sleep in Azadeh's room. She can bunk with Mona tonight." She nudged Azadeh with her arm. "Take the boy upstairs."

I grabbed my tea, and Azadeh and I walked down the narrow hallway. The walls were pretty barren compared to my house. A few family photos taken in Iran were strung up on them, one with Azadeh on the shoulders of a man with a soft smile and warm eyes like hers. Her father. A small Persian rug hung on the wall. That was another thing I found fascinating: Persians didn't walk on their rugs; they displayed them like art. Right by Azadeh's door was another piece of art with a page torn from a book detailing a photo of Persepolis and a quote:

All men have their frailties, and whoever looks for a friend without imperfections will never find what he seeks.

She opened the door, and I felt like Dorothy seeing Oz for the first time. The bed was a humble single, with a thick, big, blue blanket thrown over it. Unlike other girls' rooms, hers didn't have a heap of pillows. There

114

was only one. Practical. The room was empty other than the shelves that housed books. Out of all the books, which were in English, one had Perso-Arabic script outfacing with intricate art on the cover.

I pointed toward the mammoth book. "What's that one about?"

"The Shahnameh," she said, her face radiating pride. "The book of kings. You can't call yourself Persian and not own a copy."

"Why is it so important?"

"That book saved the Persian language. It's become a symbol of the perseverance of the Persian people and our language."

"Have you read it all? Looks thick."

"Some. It's a hard book to read. Kind of written like The Fairy Queen by Edmund Spencer. My goal is to read and understand the entirety at least once before I die."

"What's The Fairy Queen?" I asked.

She laughed. "I love that about you."

My brain froze. Love? Azadeh loved something about me. Wait, what did she love? "What? What do you love about me?"

"So many guys pretend they know everything, even when they don't. They act like they do or fake it. You don't do that. Being around you is easy because you're so genuine."

I shrugged. "Fadat besham, Azizam."

Azadeh's face flushed red. Bright red. I frowned. I was pretty sure I'd said the words right. Oh. My. God. Did I just ask her to suck my dick? Fuck.

"Um, my Persian sucks. Did I pronounce something wrong? I could've. Whatever you think I said, I didn't. I've been learning, and it's way harder than English. Did you know there's no gender? That part is kind of cool. Of course, you know that. Why wouldn't you know that?"

Azadeh grabbed my shoulders as she belly laughed. I think she snorted. Oh, my God, she thought I was a tool.

"Relax, Zeke. You didn't say anything bad. It was super sweet, even if you didn't intend to say the words. You told me you'd sacrifice your life for me."

I'd never been the praying type, but at that moment, I wanted to get down on my knees and thank baby Jesus. Profusely. "I would. I'd sacrifice my life for you, Az. No questions asked.

Azadeh framed my face, holding me still, consuming me with the need to be in her presence. At that moment, I knew I could deal with all the shitty things life threw at me as long as I had her.

Not knowing what came over me, I wrapped my arms around her and pulled her to me. We stood there for a moment, staring at each other. It was like a movie montage with music when the two characters are twirled into a sky full of stars. Being around Azadeh made me believe I was invincible. Without hesitation, I lowered my head and brushed my lips with hers.

The kiss was slow at first, tiny sparks igniting, but then my hands were in her hair, and our tongues were dancing. Fuck. I felt like I'd won the lottery. If I died and her lips were the last thing I tasted, I'd consider it a life well lived.

When we pulled back, I was so mesmerized I couldn't stop staring at her.

Her fingers moved to her lips. "That was my first kiss."

"I know you need more than I'll ever be able to give you. But I'm glad you gave me something as memorable as your first kiss." I swear the pain my father had inflicted vanished as Azadeh smiled at me.

"You're so beautiful. Sometimes, it hurts to look at you."

Azadeh's smile grew. "That's an interesting compliment. And you're more than enough for anyone. You're Ezekiel Summers, the boy who showed me that kindness can be found in the most unlikely places."

"You blind me, Az. In your presence, I'm both David and Goliath. I can't explain it. I've never met anyone like you, and I'm positive I never will again. You bewitch me in so many ways."

"We better get you to bed before my mother checks on us." Azadeh brushed past me and went to the bed, turning it down.

On her nightstand lay a battered copy of The Handmaid's Tale. The cover was dented, pages dog-eared, and highlighter applied to various paragraphs. The book was the only one in her collection that looked banged up. Most of the others on her shelf didn't even have a cracked spine.

"What's your obsession with this book?"

Azadeh pulled the book from my grasp and glided her fingers over the cover. "I find it fascinating that a woman who lived on the other side of the planet captured the horrors that haunt so many women in Iran so clearly."

"But your mom is a fierce, independent woman. She had an education, and judging by how she talks about your father, she seemed to run that show. In The Handmaid's Tale, the women are prisoners in a patriarchal nightmare. Is Iran that bad?"

Azadeh gazed at the book, her mind going to some place darker. "Like you said earlier, life is based on luck. My mother was lucky to be born to a man who respected her and lucky enough to fall in love with my father, a man who adored her. But for many women in Iran, it's like living in hell on earth, where they're nothing but property and cattle to be bartered. So your answer about Iran will depend on who you ask."

Chapter 13

Cyrus Age 30
Present Day

I'm not sure if I should invite Lev. Usually, the asshole watches us fuck, but I feel like he should be punished. I mean, we could be humping like rabbits during this visit, but now we gotta go kill some motherfuckers, thanks to Lev.

"You coming, Lev? Or are you going to watch through your cameras?" Azadeh asks.

Cameras? What does she mean, cameras? "What cameras?"

Azadeh turns to me. "You didn't know? Lev has cameras in every room and all over the property."

Lev's face goes stark white. The dude is pretty white to begin with, borderline vampire white, but now he looks like a sheet of paper.

"How did you know about that?" Lev asks.

I'm sure he thinks he was a super sleuth. I guess he was. I didn't know about it. But I'm no genius like Azadeh. The girl is as smart as a whip.

"Whoa, whoa, whoa." I jump out of my chair, letting it fall onto the marble floor. "What the fuck do you mean, cameras everywhere? Shit, Lev, you know you've always got an open invitation to at least watch."

Lev remains silent. I'd keep my mouth shut, too, if it came out that I'd been pervert peeping on my friends. He doesn't have to watch like a fucking creeper. He's watched me bang other people before. I always wondered if being a voyeur was his thing. Maybe it's his thing a little too much. I've done some fucked up shit in this house and on the grounds. And homeboy over here has the video evidence? I'm fucking pissed.

"Your freaking ass better delete me off all those videos, motherfucker."

The asshole has the nerve not even to address me. All he seems to care about is what Azadeh thinks. Can't blame him. She looks fine as hell with those leather pants that grip her curves. Her body's fire. Like, fucking perfect. The way that top hugs her tits so tightly, they're almost spilling out. Fuck, I want to bite them. She'd look so hot if she let me brand her flesh. I asked her if she would a few years ago, and she said yes when she agreed to be mine. Girl fucks my brains out but won't settle down. Who needs more than three men? We would be her fucking slaves if she said yes. Even Lev's stupid ass. He's so fucking obsessed with her.

"Hey, asshole!" I shout at Lev, forcing his attention to me. "Does she know you follow her around the globe? Or that you have a tracker in her car?"

"You have a what?" Azadeh asks through gritted teeth.

Her arms are straight by her side as she clenches her fists. She looks pissed. The sex is gonna be good. She gets crazy when she fucks mad. Like, batshit. God, I hope she pulls the knife on me.

"I wanted to make sure you were safe," Lev whispers.

"Safe?" Azadeh demands. "*Safe?* I'm a black belt with levels. I've trained with the best martial artists in the world. You couldn't keep me safe if I had a red blinking nose. You couldn't even keep Mona safe, and she's defenseless."

She cuts Lev off as he goes to respond. "Why did Mona run off on you, anyway? She knows who you are. Been around you for ten years. She'd have no reason to believe you'd harm her." She grips the handle of her knife. She has Lev on the floor before Zeke and I can do anything. She straddles him, holding the blade of her hunting knife to his jugular. "Why wasn't she feeling safe, Lev?"

My cock being hard as steel is a little fucked up. Part of me chants, "Do it! Cut him!"

"Az!" Zeke yells, his arms around her waist as he attempts to yank her off Lev.

"Why did she run off, Lev?" Azadeh screams as Zeke pulls her off.

I glance at Lev. He's almost comatose; his eyes focused on the ceiling above him, his body frozen in shock as a few drops of blood trickle from his neck onto the floor by his shoulder.

Azadeh kicks her feet, connecting with Lev's thigh. She's fuckin' lost it. The last time I saw her like this was when she attacked the leader of a sex trafficking ring. She was cold and collected one minute, and the next, she went full banshee on the guy, gutting him like a fish.

I step toward Lev and nudge him with the toe of my boot. "Get the fuck up."

Lev doesn't move. His eyes are empty as if he's fuckin' disappeared somewhere.

Like the first time I saw him.

Chapter 14

Cyrus   Age 19

Youth Psychiatric Detention Center

"**Y**o, why the fuck is that guy staring at us?" Zeke asked, peering over my shoulder.

I turned to see a guy with jet-black hair and steely eyes. "Wanna give him something to stare at?"

"It's fuckin' weird," Zeke said, ignoring my question. "He's just fucking staring at us. I'm not sure if he's even blinked."

We were in the visitor room, waiting for Azadeh. She came by twice a week. At first, it was to visit Zeke, but I'd somehow wangled an invitation to sit with them. I wanted to know what was so special about this chick Zeke was obsessed with. He cared more about her than he probably did about breathing. Shit, the girl was probably the air he inhaled.

I didn't have any problems fooling around with Zeke because he swore up and down that they were friends. He admitted he wanted more, but Azadeh refused to commit. I told him he better be upfront with me, or he'd see the full extent of my anger because we all knew I would literally burn the bitch. Turned out I had nothing to worry about because, after three months, I was halfway in love with Azadeh.

"Hi, sorry I'm late," Azadeh's soft voice chimed as she sat beside us. She had a giant beach bag with her, full to the brim. "I brought you all some stuff."

Azadeh unloaded it on the table. Rice, a stew she called Gromeh Sabzi—the stuff looked appetizing, and I swore the flavors created a party in your mouth. Who would've thought that a beef and bean stew marinated for hours in various herbs would be so fucking tasty?

I grabbed one of the paper plates Azadeh placed on the table and dug in. "When I get fat, you better still love me."

Azadeh laughed. "Be around a Persian girl, and you'll always be fed and then some." She turned her gaze on Zeke and placed her hand on his right eye. She always did that, hoping it would miraculously return to normal.

"How are you doing, Az?" Zeke asked, popping a spoonful of pomegranate in his mouth.

I liked how Azadeh removed all the seeds and put them in a Tupperware. I was lucky if my mom let me eat and this girl had brought a full meal to lockup for us.

"I'll be better once's you're out of here," she said.

"A few more months. The lawyer says I'm lucky. Getting locked up right before I turn eighteen should've gotten me a prison term instead of juvie." Zeke shrugged. "It could've been worse, Az."

Azadeh sighed, and her shoulders relaxed as she gazed at us. "Better eat up. You know how much I hate leftovers. I wish they'd let you take it back with you. It's just food. What are you gonna do, shank someone to death with some basmati rice?"

I slapped my hand over my mouth so I didn't spray food everywhere. Azadeh was something. The girl came off as this sweet, meek little thing scared of her own shadow, but she was a spitfire. Zeke once told me that she was the strongest person he knew. I tried to pry information out of him, but he told me it wasn't his story to tell, and she'd confide in me when she was ready.

I swallowed and tilted my head toward her. "You know a lot about shanking."

She smiled. "Probably more than an eighteen-year-old should."

The girl was beautiful. My hand moved instinctively to my face, and I traced the brutal burn marks. Disfigured flesh was all I presented in the world.

"They're interesting," Azadeh said as if reading my mind. She pointed to my face when I glanced at her. "Your scars are interesting."

"They make me look like a monster," I said, eyes connecting with hers.

"No, they don't. Monsters are beautiful, Cyrus. You should know that. They appeal to the masses. Their beauty lulls you into a sense of safety. If demons showed you their true face, they couldn't corrupt innocent people." She placed her hand on my cheek. "You, above all others, understand the tragedy of what a real monster is capable of."

A lump formed in my throat, and my mouth went dry. She held me in a tender moment, and I didn't do sweet moments well. It was why I used humor so much. The laughing lunatic. A model after the Joker from Batman. Let them think you were crazy. I was the *epitome of the graphic novel The Killing Joke by Alan Moore.*

Screams startled us, and we turned to see the guy with the black hair and creepy eyes on the ground. He was like a wild animal, lashing out, his teeth digging into the hand of one of the guards. Fuck, that dude was going to get it. They'd probably drug him and leave him drooling in a locked room somewhere. His screams were shrill and terrifying. That wasn't a sound a man made from being jumped. It stemmed from something else. It was almost like he was being subjected to the most gruesome form of torture.

Before I could stop her, Azadeh was on her feet, running toward him. I moved to follow, but Zeke grabbed my hand. "Sit down."

"Sit down? Bro, she's about to enter a war zone."

Zeke chuckled. "She's a black belt in a few different martial arts. She could probably take down the guards and the lunatic. Besides, if you try to play the savior, she'll get pissed and probably never make you food again."

I had no idea how Zeke was so calm with Azadeh throwing herself among a bunch of grown men with copious amounts of adrenaline flowing through their systems. "If she gets hurt, I'll fuck your ass without lube."

Zeke laughed. "If she gets it sorted without bloodshed, I'll fuck your ass with lube because I'm not a psycho, unlike you. But I won't let you come for a week."

My eyes narrowed. "Bet."

Azadeh reached the guards. They said something to each other before she crouched by the black-haired guy. He thrashed and bared his teeth at her. It took everything in me not to go over and kick his ass. But thirty minutes later, the most fucked up thing happened. The guards backed off, and he followed her back to our table.

"Guys, this is Lev," Azadeh said as if we were at a picnic and she was introducing us to a new friend. "Lev doesn't like to be touched. I need the two of you to make sure everyone knows that."

Zeke smiled and moved over, making room for Azadeh's new stray. "Hey, man. I'm Zeke, and that one is Cyrus. Nice to meet you."

The Lev guy didn't say anything. He sat with his head hanging.

"You hungry, Lev?" Azadeh asked as she grabbed a paper plate and filled it with the food meant for us.

"We share our food with the stray too?" I asked, annoyed. *"You know if you feed them, they keep coming back."*

Azadeh raised her right eyebrow. "Cyrus, should you be casting stones when you were brought into the inner circle the same way?"

"Yes. I told you, feed a stray, and they keep coming back." I turned to Lev. "So why don't you like to be touched?"

"Why do you have those hideous marks on your face?" Lev parried.

Fuckin' smart ass. "Parents."

"Same."

Chapter 15

Lev   Age 30
Present Day

I consider myself an intelligent man. Or I did until I came up with an idiotic scheme to kidnap Mona. I figured everything would go smoothly, and we'd finally have Azadeh home. Never in a million years did I think my plan would be flipped on its head.

She should've stabbed that blade into my jugular. Put me out of my damn misery. I grind my teeth as my rage ignites. None of this would've happened if she'd come home as promised. I can give her everything she wants. She says she wants her freedom, but we never held her in a cage. The manor could be her home base while she continued to save her lost souls. Fuck, doesn't she get that her job with the three of us isn't complete? Who leaves a project half-done?

At least I'm bleeding on the marble. That's easy enough to clean up. It could've been on the Persian carpets. I only bought those carpets for Azadeh. They were supposed to be hung on the walls. I got pissed and put them on the floor. I also wear shoes in the house because it irritates her.

How did she find out about the surveillance?

She's lucky you didn't put one under her skin.

I shut my eyes, trying to block out that voice. It's the same fuckin' voice that tempted me to drug her evening tea so I could sneak into her room and defile her. I thought that was a one-and-done, but nothing is that simple for an addict. Especially when they're given the best fucking high of their life. She'd kill me if she saw the videos. But it's the only way I can touch her. I try to fight that voice, but occasionally I can't. Guess it's in my DNA. Mother only loved me when I was a good boy, and Father only loved me when she did.

Zeke is by my side. He mumbles something I can't make out while holding his hands out to me. We've been working on my issues for a couple of years, and for the most part, I was getting better. In the beginning, his touch was like being encased naked in an icy casket, but now I can somewhat tolerate it. At least my brain doesn't recoil, leaving me an empty husk. We decided to keep it a secret, not wanting to let the others know until I had it under control.

I don't understand why I have such an aversion to touch. I never cared about my little issue until I fell in love with three misfits who gave me my first taste of family. Shit, before these three, I assumed love was your mother forcing you to watch the defilement of screaming children. The woman held me to her, lovingly brushing my hair out of my face as she told me how much she loved me and was glad I'd never be one of those boys. The nightmares from those screams still wake me at night in a cold sweat.

When the cops found me curled in a ball, rocking back and forth, bloody knife in my hand beside my mother's mangled body, which was slashed like a pinata, they thought I was the next Edmund Kepner. A serial killer. They were half right. I *am* a killer, and my moral compass is skewed at best, but there's nothing serial about me.

The evening sun sets, and the seductive allure of dusk shrouds the manor. The floor-to-ceiling windows are a nice touch. Azadeh once complained that the manor was a stuffy crypt and needed light. That forced me to demolish the stone at the back of the house and install glass walls.

My body stiffens as Zeke brushes his fingers against me.

"Take a breath," Zeke says, leaving one hand on my arm while ensuring the other is visible.

He's using the method we've been working on. He touches me casually to allow my brain to register that he's safe. That *I'm* safe. I force myself to make eye contact with him. Shutting out the world and seeing only him. Zeke. He's my safety point. He'll never harm me. I'm safe.

He must recognize something in my eyes because he asks a simple question. "Feel better?"

"Better? Not sure. But I can handle it."

"Did you go there?" Zeke asks.

I nod. It's the only place I go. My mother's beaming smile as she watches other people's children brutalized in ungodly ways. I always see her. But oddly, it isn't the torture that makes my stomach churn. What damages me the most is my mother's joy as she watches the horror before her.

I shudder at the memory. I want to scrub it from my brain, but I never can. I try to focus on the comfort of Zeke's arm instead of the horrified cries of the children burned into my memory.

I shut my eyes, concentrating on Zeke's touch and the warmth of his deep voice.

My eyes fly open, and a vivid blue eye captures mine. Zeke's face is scrunched with concern, marring his Hollywood star looks. He's so handsome. It's a pity he doesn't realize the truth of his beauty. He believes the eye patch detracts from his attractiveness, but it only adds to it. An air of danger on the most angelic face I've ever seen.

"Fuck," Azadeh mumbles, rushing to my side. Tears well in her deep brown eyes. "Lev, I'm sorry."

She's apologizing to me? I'm the idiot who kidnapped her sister and lost her because I couldn't vocalize my needs like a normal person. Mona is in danger because of me. Azadeh should be slitting my throat, not kneeling by my side, crying. The capacity of love in her heart is inconceivable. Her limitless kindness consumes me. Her sweet soul pushes me to the brink of madness.

"You're the air I breathe, Azadeh," I whisper so low that I'm not sure she hears me. "You can't fault a man for doing what's necessary to keep his life safe."

My words are a half-truth because my actions aren't solely to protect her; they're about my obsession with her—an obsession that borders on sickness.

An obsession that disgusts even me.

Chapter 16

Lev   Age 23
The Manor

I had no clue why I kept the manor. The place was a haunted hell of brutal memories and horror. I longed to strip bare and drain every ounce of my parents' DNA from my body. But since that wasn't possible, I erased their essence from the house they'd loved. I hired a company and used the money I inherited from the animals to eliminate their presence. The house had morphed from an ancient mausoleum into a modern haven.

I gazed at the state-of-the-art surveillance system. A camera covered each room, every hallway, corner, and inch of land. I'd set them up for safety, that little boy inside me still paranoid about the boogeyman coming to get me. But that all changed the night I saw Azadeh naked in her bed.

Many beautiful women had been written about in history. Some caused the downfall of empires. Others the beheading of great rulers. I'd always dismissed those tales as fodder spun by misogynistic men who feared the fairer sex. But as I gazed at Azadeh's sleeping form, her large breasts rising and falling in a slow rhythm, I knew I would do anything for one taste. The only problem was that my broken and battered mind wouldn't allow anything to come to fruition in a healthy way.

I envied how Zeke, Cyrus, and Azadeh touched each other. How they physically demonstrated their love and connection was a foreign entity to me. Something peculiar and strange to my genetic makeup. The idea of one of them accidentally grazing my flesh made my skin crawl and my mind recoil. When Zeke and I worked on my issues with touch, it was controlled. I knew what was coming and prepared for it, but I wasn't at a place where it was remotely natural to be touched by another.

I didn't know why I left the surveillance room and walked to Azadeh's door that night. The yearning to be close to her overpowered all my logic. My actions were devoid of moral credibility, but I didn't care. My hands shook as I grabbed the gold handle and twisted, opening her bedroom door. I could've stopped there. Had I done so, I wouldn't have gained an addiction that would plague me for years to come. A burning desire that I would never rid myself of and would push me to more disgusting acts.

I scanned the room. Perfectly clean and painfully minimalist, it was like a vacant space housing someone for a night. A pit stop on her journey to her final destination.

Azadeh slept peacefully as I crept into the room and walked toward her in the center of the king-size bed. My fingers itched to touch her long black hair, which fanned over the pillow. A fucking angel tempting the devil himself. Closing my eyes, I inhaled the soft scent that was distinctively hers, infiltrating the room. Jasmine. A sweet floral note with a hint of a deadly musk. I smiled at how perfectly her perfume captured her personality. My sweet Azadeh, who could slice open a man's throat without blinking.

The blanket shifted, exposing her bare leg. Her thick, silky-soft thighs were a glimpse into the untold universe of pleasure her body offered. A world I'd never allow myself to access in the light of day. But at night, under the shroud of shadow and the shimmering moonlight filtering through the window, my situation transformed, offering enticement wrapped in a shiny red bow.

I glanced at the clothes discarded by the bed. A crimson t-shirt, black pants, and...undergarments. A black satin bra with matching boy-cut shorts. Of course, Azadeh wouldn't be a thong girl. She was too practical for barely there scraps of fabric.

I bent and picked up the underwear, holding it in my hand. There was something primitive about holding a piece of cloth that had touched her most sensitive flesh. Raising the garment to my face, I inhaled her scent, letting it drown my lungs and take over my mind. I loathed the reality that made pathetic moments like these all I would ever have of her. I was a bystander to my existence.

The duvet shifted again, exposing more of her alluring flesh. What would she taste like? Would the touch of her skin burn like I'd conjured in my mind, or would it be a salve that healed my mangled heart? During all the years I'd known Azadeh, I'd never dreamed of a moment when I could be with her without battling the fortress my mind had built to protect me.

I had a profound understanding that my desires were fundamentally wrong. I knew as I reached out to touch her flesh that I was giving in to darkness. But what was someone to do when the only thing that could bring them salvation was giving in to their depraved needs? I'd lived in damnation my entire exis-

tence. I understood that when I died, my soul would rot in the fiery pits of hell. But for one moment, I longed for a reprieve from the ravenous demons roaring in my soul.

I pressed Azadeh's underwear to my nose and inhaled again, submerging myself in what I longed for most in the world before stuffing them in my pants pocket like a pervert. But the need to down myself in her wasn't satiated. I wanted more.

Moving my eyes from her sleeping, I saw the bottle of Benadryl on the nightstand. My desperate need for her drove my next thought. I lifted the cover, exposing her slightly parted legs. I took in her pretty pink pussy, and my mouth watered at the thought of one small taste. I knew what I was about to do was wrong, but I did it anyway.

Falling to my knees, I moved closer to her core, placing my nose against her. Fuck, her scent was far sweeter when inhaled from the source. I pressed my face closer to paradise. The panties in my pocket were cut cocaine, but her cunt was pure fish scale. Addicts would kill for one taste.

I rubbed my nose between her pussy lips. Part of me was afraid she'd open her eyes, and terror would spark in those perfect molten dark brown eyes. When she continued to slumber, my bravery peaked. Using my fingers, I parted her, sliding the tip of my tongue along her sensitive flesh. Fuck! Her intoxicating flavor tantalized my taste buds. I knew I was done for. A profound knowledge seeped into every fiber of my being—this would be my dirty little secret and something I'd never be able to abstain from.

Azadeh rustled the sheets as her legs opened wider, inviting my tongue to delve deeper. Like an addict staring at a bag of narcotics, I dived in, not worrying about the repercussions of my actions.

"You taste so good, pretty girl. Even better than I dreamed," I murmured as I licked her slit.

Azadeh's moans played in surround sound, an opus in a cinematic production, alluding to an upcoming climax. My need for her consumed me. I'd forgotten how to be preoccupied with the realities of life.

Chapter 17

Azadeh   Age 29

Present Day

Lev's words linger between us, causing a poisonous thickness in the air.

You can't fault a man for doing what's necessary to keep his life safe.

I said something similar to him three months ago when I told him I'd forgive anything. Perhaps that statement was a lie, but I sure believed it at the time. But as I stand here, I'm torn between my love for him and my anger. I love him so much that I'd die for him. But he crossed a line and put my sister, my blood, at risk. If anything happens to Mona, I don't think I'll ever be able to look at Lev again.

They say that love breaks your heart, but in reality, it breaks your brain. Your heart is a functional organ that pumps blood, but your brain? Your brain is the organ that twists you up so completely, you break in a million different ways. That's why I've always thought the expression "broken heart" is idiotic. A broken heart means you're dead. Broken hearts don't bring about suffering; they bring about morbid relief.

The whole time I was driving up here, I considered different scenarios and their outcomes. I asked myself why Lev would do what he did. Lev, a man I opened my heart and my life to. A man who sat at my maman's dinner table, eating heaps of food while smiling at her. The same guy who paid for my sister's expensive college tuition when I didn't have the money.

Lev has always taken care of my family and me without me having to ask him for anything. Never in a million years did I think he'd cause my world to crash around me one day.

I take in Lev's frantic state. His breathing is labored, and his eyes are wild as they flit around the room until they finally land on me.

"I'm so fuckin' sorry. I can't pretend I didn't know what I was doing because I did. At first, I was fine when you were in Asia, but I panicked when you were in Tehran. I'd made connections there over the years and had them keeping an eye on you."

There's no way Lev would know I was in Iran. I didn't have my car there, and it's not like he had a tracker under my skin. His eyes flicker to the Farvahar necklace on my neck. I never take it off. Usually, it's hidden under my clothes, but I even shower with the piece.

I reach for the necklace and clasp it. "You put a tracker in my necklace?"

Lev looks sheepish, averting his gaze to the expensive Italian marble floors.

"But I've had this since I turned nineteen. I wasn't even doing anything dangerous then. At that time, the plan was to go to med school."

"It didn't matter," Lev whispers. "I have a sickness. I'm a virus that needs containment before I spread. The only person who's ever made me feel safe is you. As long as I know you're okay, I'm okay. I told you years ago, Az, I'm not a normal man. My sickness is in my DNA."

I want to rip the necklace off and gouge out his eyes with the wings of the Farvahar. Not because he's controlled me when he knows how much my autonomy means to me, but because of his self-deprecation. A part of me wants to lash out and tell him to suck it up, to be an adult. But I don't. "You know what the problem is between us, Lev?"

His gaze bolts from the floor to focus on me. He's no longer sheepish as his eyes narrow and his hands form fists at his sides.

"There is no problem between us," he grits between clenched teeth.

"Buddy, have you forgotten you kidnapped her sister?" Cyrus states the obvious behind me. "I'd say that's a pretty fucking big problem."

Ignoring Cyrus, I focus on Lev. "The problem is that I gave you my trust foolishly, and you withheld yours willingly."

I rise and leave the room, leaving Lev crumpled on the floor.

"No," I hear Zeke say behind me. "You've done enough. I'll take care of it."

I open the door to my room, unsure I can call it "mine" now that a part of me feels like I've been living a lie. I glance at the wall where a giant mural hangs from ceiling to floor. Persepolis. I smile, remembering how Cyrus worked painstakingly on the piece for months. He'd growled at me when I told him we could get a print. He'd explained that having an artist madly in love with me meant he would paint anything I desired anytime I wanted. Three months later, he covered my eyes and revealed his masterpiece.

I trace the pillars with my fingertips, gazing at the bright blue horizon painted at the top close to the ceiling.

I'm startled by the knock at my door. Turning, I see Zeke poking his head in.

"I should've been content with you giving me my tattoo," I say with a huff before bouncing my butt on the bed.

Zeke smiles as he sits beside me. We don't say anything for a long while as we stare at the mural.

"That was a good birthday," I say, finally breaking the silence.

"It sure was." Zeke chuckles.

I glare at him, gently shoving his shoulder. "I'm serious."

"So am I. It's not every day you get to go down on your soulmate."

My hand moves to the delicate emblem on the gold chain. "Why'd he have to use this?"

Zeke sighs. "Because he knew you wouldn't take it off. As long as that necklace was moving, so were you."

"That's idiotic because someone could've stolen it. It could've been moving while I lay dismembered in a ditch somewhere."

"He probably would've embedded it under your skin, but he knew you'd kick his ass." Zeke laughs. "But in all seriousness, Az, you're pretty hard to kill, and he knew that. Did you ever have a security object as a kid?"

I glare at him. "Yes, a doll named Parvaneh."

"You named your doll butterfly?"

"It's also a name in Iran."

"Anyways. Do you remember how Parvaneh made you feel?"

I smiled sadly. "Yes, I loved that thing. I had that doll until my early teens. When we had to leave, I sobbed, knowing I'd have to leave it behind."

"Why'd you leave it?"

I glare at him as if he's asked the most moronic thing in the world. Then I realize that most people don't understand what happens with immigration and how no one wants to leave their home. People leave because they have to, not because they want to. "We ran in the middle of the night and trekked through a desert to get into Pakistan. We only packed essentials, and unfortunately, a doll took up room that could be used for food and clothes."

Zeke nods. "Remember how you felt when you couldn't take her?"

"Yes, I was pretty devastated. But the marks on my back forced me to get over it quickly."

"I could cover them up for you." Zeke's hand automatically moves to my back, and he places it over my scars. "You're not betraying anyone by being happy,"

I've thought about getting a tattoo over my lash marks—something to hide the humiliation and pain. But over the years, I've come to regard them as a reminder of how lucky I was. "No. I need them. If I cover them up, I'm covering the others—the ones who got the seventy-two lashes and were raped or murdered for not bending. I won't erase them by erasing those marks." I place my hand on his cheek, and his eyes shutter closed. "Go on about your security blanket analogy."

"Comfort object," Zeke corrects. "The point is that you, Azadeh Baran, are Lev's comfort object. He needs to know you're safe and sound so he can sleep at night. So give him a little grace because I'm fairly confident he could take his madness to much greater depths."

Chapter 18

Zeke   Age 20

The Guys first apartment together

"**T**his look all right?" Cyrus asked for the hundredth time as he ran out of his room.

He was wearing the most un-Cyrus-like suit. Black, sleek, and professional. I was in the Twilight Zone because Cyrus wore ripped jeans and hoodies so much that it was a uniform.

I burst out laughing. "Did you raid Lev's closet?"

"Maybe. Mothers like this shit. It makes me appear like I'm not a loser and can take care of her daughter."

"Where did you hear that?" I asked between bouts of laughter.

"The Shahs of Sunset," Cyrus said, tugging his tie. "They said presentation is everything. I thought my *parents were high-maintenance, but Persian parents are no joke. The dad on that show got upset about his kid ending up with a man who only made six figures."*

"Azadeh hates that show. She says it's a farce. If I remember correctly, she told me those people know nothing about Iran or the Persian identity other than eating koobideh, owning a Persian cat, and showing off some handmade silk carpets."

I brought my focus back to the mirror and brushed my unruly mop to the side. "Mrs. Baran isn't like that. She let Azadeh visit us in juvie, remember? Not just any juvie either, one for the criminally insane."

I still couldn't believe Azadeh had visited me every Sunday for two years. I was sure Nasrin would've put a stop to that, but to my surprise, Azadeh had shown up with food like clockwork.

"Yeah, I guess that's true. You can't be that stuck up if you let your teen daughter hang out with murderers and nutjobs."

"Are you ready?" Lev asked, leaning against the door-frame in a dark navy three-piece suit.

I scanned his thick frame, focusing on his medium-brown Italian leather loafers. "Remember to remove your shoes once you get to the door."

I walked over to Cyrus, loosened his crooked tie, and removed it. "Don't worry. Nasrin Baran always sat at the kitchen table while I was in her daughter's room. You're freaking yourself out way more than you need to."

* * *

*"Y**ou okay? You look like you're about to throw up," Lev said as I rang the doorbell.*

My hands were clammy, and my body was restless. I'd been to this house many times, slept on the sofa, Azadeh's bed, and in Dariyus's room once he went to college, but I still experienced a sense of unease about coming back here after I was locked up. It was almost as if I would suddenly be unwelcome.

Mona opened the door, and before she said anything, she leaped into my arms. "Zeke. I'm so happy to see you. I wanted to visit you when you were in jail, but Maman said it was no place for a young girl. I pointed out that Azadeh was a young girl, but that only made her cock an eyebrow and tell me I was a Bache pourroh."

I hugged Mona fiercely, shocked at how much I'd missed her. Being six years Azadeh's junior, Mona had also become a kid sister to me. "It's good to see you, Azizam, chegat gondeh shodi."

"Ah, man, you speaking Farsi too, now? Maman says I need to speak Farsi at home so I don't lose it. I'm not sure why I need to know it anyway. It's not like it's gonna do anything for me. It's only spoken in three countries, and then random diaspora."

"There's one very valid reason to learn it." I bent and handed her the smaller package by my feet.

Mona tapped my shoulder to be let down before ripping into her present.

"Two questions," Cyrus whispered in my ear. "One, what did you say to her, and two, was I supposed to bring the kid a present?"

"I called her sweetheart and told her she got big," I murmured. "I always get her something, but you don't have to."

"Yes, he does," Mona said, squealing as she held up an iPhone. "Oh, my God, Zeke! This is the best present ever." Mona threw her arms around me, giving me a fierce hug.

"It's already set up, and I put you on my plan, but go easy on the data, will you? I know how crazy thirteen-year-olds are."

"Mona, let them in," Mrs. Baran said as she shuffled toward the door. As soon as she saw me, she shrieked and threw her arms around me like her youngest daughter. "Ah, Joonam. Mard shodi." My life. You've become a man.

I wrapped my arms around her, allowing myself to be swallowed in her warmth.

She pulled away and brought her hands to my face, pulling my head down and kissing my forehead. "Please, come in."

I bent to pick up the giant box before we went inside. We removed our shoes in the entryway and followed Nasrin into the house.

"Where's Azadeh?" I asked, putting my present on the dining room table.

"She's right here," Azadeh said from behind me.

I turned, and my eye nearly popped out of my head. If this were a teen movie montage from the nineties, the scene would be in slow motion, and a divine light would shroud my girl's head.

I didn't wait for her to reach the bottom of the stairs before I rushed to her, wrapping my arms around her waist and picking her up. Bending my head to her ear, I whispered so only she could hear,

"You look beautiful, aziz-e-delam." Dearest to my heart.

Azadeh's cheeks flushed pink. "Thank you."

Cyrus tugged at my arms. "Stop hogging her." He pulled me off her and gave her a quick squeeze. "Tavalodat Mobarack."

Azadeh and I were taken aback by Cyrus's attempt at Farsi as he wished her a happy birthday.

He smirked at us. "You're not the only one who watches YouTube videos. Those old Persian movies are pretty dope. That Fardin guy was a looker, huh? The Paul Newman of Iran, I'd say."

Azadeh giggled. "He's my maman's favorite."

"What's my favorite?" Nasrin asked as she poked her head out of the kitchen.

"Cyrus here likes Fardin movies," Azadeh explained.

Nasrin wiped her hands on her apron and walked over to us. She took Cyrus's hand and dragged him away. "You have to tell me which one. I have all of his movies on VHS."

Azadeh and I laughed as we walked over to Lev, sitting by the sofa with a cup of cardamom tea in his hand and a lollipop stick standing up in it.

He raised the cup to us, his thumb squished in the ridiculously tiny handle. "Your mother has filled this up three times in the last thirty minutes. It would make more sense if she gave me a coffee mug." He pulled out the lollipop stick. "This is the most delightful sugar I've ever had, but what are these red things floating inside?"

"I thought you were rich," I said, sitting beside him. "Don't you know those red things are more expensive than gold?"

Azadeh rolled her eyes at me before turning to Lev. "It's saffron."

Lev placed the cup on the table and rose from his seat as if realizing he should've said hello to Azadeh before mindlessly insulting her maman's tea. His hand disappeared into his coat pocket, and he pulled out a small velvet box.

"You're not proposing to her, are you?" Cyrus asked as he entered the modest living room, holding a giant bowl of fruit with small cucumbers hanging over the side. "I like the little cucumbers. Nasrin says they're Persian." Cyrus glanced at Azadeh. "And we all know how much I love Persian things."

"Cucumbers are a fruit, so it's appropriate," Lev said.

"Azadeh, Mona, help me set the table," Nasrin called from the kitchen. "Make sure our guests eat. Tarof bokon."

Azadeh rolled her eyes. "Help yourselves, but don't eat too much and get full. If you don't eat Maman's food, she'll be insulted."

* * *

An hour later, we finished our third helping. As soon as our plates were empty, Nasrin had filled them again. Even with the copious amounts the three of us ate, there were still leftovers.

"What's this salad?" Cyrus asked as he loaded his plate. "I grew up with only Caesar and garden. If my mother had made this one, I wouldn't have kicked and screamed to avoid it."

Nasrin beamed at him. "It's called salad Shirazi."

I couldn't believe how easily he'd won her over by complimenting her food. Her food was good, mind you. It was probably the best cuisine I'd ever sampled. Nasrin ate up every compliment Cyrus threw at her. The way she gazed at him like he was her long-lost baby boy was astounding. But that was how she made everyone feel, as if they were a member of her family.

"Cyrus, I meant to ask you. Are you Persian?"

"Me?" Cyrus asked. "No, I wish, though, because Persian moms can cook. I love that you use a spoon more than a fork. Most things fall off my fork. It makes way more sense to eat rice with a spoon." He demonstrated his appreciation of Nasrin's culinary talents by shoving a spoonful of salad into his mouth.

"You have a very famous Persian name," Nasrin explained. "The name itself isn't Persian. We Iranians call him Koorosh."

"Cyrus the Great," Lev chipped in. "The first king of the Persian empire. We credit the man with creating the concept of human rights. I believe they called him the great liberator. It's ironic that a country that created human rights now doesn't possess any."

The table went so silent that the only intelligible sound was Cyrus chewing.

"Men like Cyrus don't come along very often," Azadeh whispered. "There's nothing wrong with obtaining power, but when it's used to subjugate, it causes a catastrophe."

Nasrin gazed up at a large framed photo of the ancient ruins of Persepolis. "Persia was meant to be a place where different ethnicities, religions, and identities lived together in harmony. Now, it's held hostage by *corrupt men and their lackeys. I've lost many things to Iran, but I haven't lost my hope that one day, it will fulfill its destiny of becoming a free society. I hope I'm alive to see it."*

Nasrin's expression morphed from sorrow to love as she looked at her daughter. "That's enough of that. It's Azadeh's birthday, a time for celebration. How about we open your gifts?" Nasrin waved me off as I stood to clear the table. "Leave it. I will take care of it later."

"You absolutely will not," I retorted. "The three of us and little Mona here will clean up while you ladies pour a cup of tea and relax."

"But you're my guest. Guests don't clean up," Nasrin huffed.

"I'm not a guest, Nasrin. You're a second mother to me. You heal me when I'm sick, comfort me when I'm hurt. You've done more for me than my own parents. Dastet dard nakoneh madar joon." May your hand not hurt, mother dearest.

I got a little choked up as Nasrin's eyes filled with tears. She placed a hand on my cheek and smiled. "You are such a sweet man, Zeke. You deserved better in life."

The guys and I cleaned up and moved into the small living room, where Mona, Azadeh, and Nasrin were waiting for us.

"So, which one is your boyfriend, Azadeh?" Nasrin asked abruptly.

The three of us froze, eyes darting everywhere in the room but at the ladies.

"All of them and none of them," Azadeh said simply. "I'm not ready to commit, but if I were, I'd never be able to choose."

Nasrin nodded and passed Azadeh the first gift. A plain white envelope. "This is from Mona and me."

Azadeh opened the card, reading silently before she hugged her mom. "Merci, Maman."

"I'll go next," I said. "That big box is from me."

"I think women prefer tiny boxes," Cyrus said, elbowing my ribs. "Those giant boxes are only cool when you're seven."

"Watch and learn, grasshopper," I replied, beaming as Azadeh opened the box and her face lit up.

Azadeh pulled out Lavashak, Iranian fruit leather, Gaz, Iranian nougat, Sohan, a type of Persian toffee with pistachios, and various other Iranian sweets and snacks. "Oh, my god, Zeke! How did you get all this?"

"I ordered it from Los Angeles. I would've also gotten you some baked goods, but I wasn't sure how they would travel. One day, we'll visit Tehrangeles. I know it's not Theran, Shiraz, or Rasht, but L.A. might fill in some of the void."

Azadeh jumped up to hug me, and I breathed in her scent. I'd never tire of how my girl smelled.

"There's one more thing in the box."

Azadeh squealed as she moved back and dug into the box, pulling out an ornate copy of The Shahnameh. She gazed at me. "Zeke, this... this is beautiful."

"Yes, yes, me next," Cyrus said, pushing past me and handing Azadeh a slender package about forty inches long.

She laughed as she swiftly untied the half-hazard bow and pulled out a Persian sabar.

"You got me a shamshir," Azadeh said in delight.

She jumped up, hugging Cyrus and almost tackling him to the floor.

Cyrus turned to Lev. "Beat that."

"I guess I'm next," Lev said, pointing to the small package. "That small one is from me."

Azadeh smiled as she abandoned her death grip on Cyrus's head. Picking up the small package, she opened it. She didn't speak, but her eyes welled up as she pulled out a long gold chain with a winged man holding ropes of some sort.

"You got me a Farvahar." She turned the pendant over. "Good thoughts. Good word. Good deeds."

Lev moved toward her, clasping the gold necklace around her neck.

"I'm never taking this off," she whispered as she touched it gently.

I leaned into Cyrus. "Guess we both lost."

Chapter 19

Cyrus – Age 30

I crack open Azadeh's bedroom door without knocking. "We're still mad at Lev, right?"

Azadeh glares at me. "Yes. Come in and close the door."

Fuck, she's so cute when she's mad. I've been thinking about all the ways I can get her to fuck me right now. Last time she was this pissed, I ended up with a bunch of scars on my thigh. You'd think I'd have an aversion to more scars, but the ones she gave me are hot as fuck. My little vampire.

I jump on the bed beside her and lean on my elbows. "I think you should ride my face while telling him he'll never be man enough for you. That seems like a good punishment."

"Do you ever not think about sex?" Zeke asks.

"Oh, hey there, Ezekiel, I didn't even see you. Do you ever get bored being a pathetic crybaby?"

Zeke jumps up and straddles my waist. His hands move to his zipper as he knees his way up the mattress until his crotch is level with my face. He pulls his dick out. "Someone should've taught you to keep your pathetic mouth shut years ago."

He leans forward and brushes the tip of his dick between my lips. My mouth opens wide, taking in his girth.

"Looks like you're the baby now, Cy, needing a big fat cock to pacify you."

I grip Zeke's hips and push him back, smiling smugly as his ass hits the floor. Tugging down my zipper, I unleash my dick, hold it in my hand and wave it at his face. "Nah, pretty boy. If anyone is going to suck on a soother tonight, it'll be you." I slap him on the face with my dick. "Say ah."

Zeke lunges and grabs my ankle, yanking me forward. I stumble and lose my balance. His hand flies to my throat and presses firmly, restricting my airway so that speaking is almost impossible. I love it when he's like this.

Most of the time, Zeke holds back, scared of what others will think of him if they discover who he truly is. Sometimes, he even hides this part from Azadeh, but this side of him has to be fed so he can hold us all together. Because we all need him to be the strong one, the kind one, the one who pushes us to be the best we can be.

Maybe that's why we all go to him first. He's the first to know our secrets and struggles and the first to hold us in the dark and tell us everything will all be okay. Every once in a while, I poke at his rage so he can unleash it and get what he desperately needs but is too frightened to ask for.

I fist my fingers in Zeke's hair, pulling at the loose strands. I yank his head until his fingers loosen on my throat, using my weight to slam his body on the floor with a thud. "Fuck you, Zeke. You want to choke me with that pathetic dick, make me."

I glance at Azadeh. Her eyes follow our every move. She likes these games, too, but when she plays, the risks escalate. She claws and punches and, on occasion, pierces skin with a blade to relish the sight of blood. For a sweet, thoughtful girl, she sure has an immense bloodlust.

I meet Azadeh's eyes, considering if I should bring her in or not. She's probably worried sick about Mona, but relieving some stress and unloading a fraction of her rage will give her clarity when we're in the thick of danger tomorrow. Oh, fuck it, the worst that can happen is I'll be in the dog house with Lev for a while. It's not like Azadeh can stay mad for long. Like a typical hot head, she boils over quickly and cools down just as fast. "It's okay, Az. I got some of this for you, too. I know how much you like being a little whore beneath me."

Zeke's fist shoots out, but before it connects with my face, he yanks my head back by my hair.

Azadeh smirks at me, her pretty lips turned up in a smile. "The only little whore I see is the one beneath me."

That's my girl.

Azadeh presses her foot against my back, and I slam to the ground face-first. "You've forgotten your manners, Cyrus. What should we do about that? Should we tie you up and make you watch as Zeke fucks me while calling you a pathetic little boy? Maybe if you beg nice and long for me, I'll let his cum drip into your pathetic cum-guzzling mouth."

Fuck. Hearing Azadeh talk like this does it for me. She's so sweet that you'd never think the girl has a depraved side, but my god, she likes to dirty talk.

"I'll be your whipping boy, Hellcat. I'll crawl on broken glass for a simple smile from you. But we both know you need to be owned like a dog tonight. You need us to shut off your mind, abuse your body, use your holes as if they mean nothing, and paint your body with cum."

Azadeh stares at me as she pulls down her pants, taking her underwear with them. She lifts her foot off me to kick them off. My gaze moves to the gates of heaven situated between her legs. If I were a dog, I'd be salivating with my tongue out.

My eyes roam from her ankles to her thighs, up the curves of her body to her beautiful face with those soulful brown eyes. Fuck, she makes me behave like a chump. I may tease Zeke for being soft around her, but Azadeh has the same effect on all of us. She takes our sharp edges and molds them until they're less dangerous.

Zeke wraps his arms around her soft belly and nuzzles her neck. The words fall so effortlessly from his lips. "You're so damn beautiful."

She smiles at his gentle touch. He's always making her smile. She finds me funny, laughing at all my jokes, and we banter, but I've never coaxed that kind of smile from her. I meant what I said to her a moment ago—I would crawl over broken glass for her smiles. Shit, I'd do anything for them.

I push back the mushy shit, needing to stay focused. Azadeh needs it fast and rough. I can give it to her. Zeke can't. He can bruise her flesh and fuck her raw, but he can't lead with filth. Not the way I can. Not the way she needs.

"We gonna fuck or not?" I ask to break up anything that could lead to realizations and grand statements of love.

Azadeh pushes me down with her foot and smiles as she peers at me. She lifts her arms, and

Zeke pulls her shirt off over her big tits, discarding it on the floor by his feet. Azadeh removes her foot from my chest and places her feet beside my head. "Oh, we'll fuck all right."

I start to speak, but my words are muffled as she lowers herself over my face, and I taste the sweetness of her pussy. There are a million ways a man can die, but being suffocated by this woman's cunt may be the ultimate way to go. That would be a bitchin obituary: *Pyromaniac Cyrus Porter Dies While Eating His Favorite Meal.*

Chapter 20

Zeke Age 29

Present Day

I used to balk at the idea of any man touching Azadeh, but then I fell in love with Cyrus, and my notion of love expanded. Love went from a possessive idea to a holistic one. No longer was it about exclusivity; instead, it formed into a community.

Love is an ocean with endless waterways.

Nasrin was the first person I willingly confided in about my sexuality. I ran to their house after my father took a baseball bat to me in another fit of rage. If that man took one thing seriously about the Bible, it was never to spare the child and constantly use the rod.

I was a scared kid, sixteen years old, confused about my urges and the homophobic rage it unleashed. Nasrin sat me down and silently cleaned my wounds with the gentle hands of a mother I'd never known until her. When she found out that my father's latest violent outburst was because of my sexuality, she wrapped her arms around me and told me about the great love between prominent Persian poets, Shams and Rumi. That conversation created a lifelong fascination and appreciation for the great Persian poets and helped shine a light into my darkest times.

Rage consumes me at what Levinston has done. He took Mona and scared her by not revealing himself, which forced her to run. Nasrin taught her daughters never to surrender. She instilled in them that it's better to die fighting than to break at the hands of a man. Lev knew Mona wouldn't wait quietly until he got what he wanted.

I glance at the corner of the room, where I figure one of Lev's cameras is placed. I hope he's watching this. "You're so fucked up, Lev," I say to the camera. "Cyrus is obsessed with fire, but you throw the lit match on everything good you've found in this miserable world."

173

I don't take my eye off the camera as I shove Azadeh forward, exposing her thick, round ass. Kneeling over Cyrus, I line up the tip of my dick before I sink into her with one full thrust. "Hope you're watching this, Lev. Spit on your hand while you sit in your office and jerk your cock, wishing it was buried deep in her pussy. Keep watching us fuck, pretending it's you."

I grip Azadeh's hair and yank her head back. Her hips circle as she attempts to get the best friction between my cock and Cyrus's face. "I hope the day you decide to join the living, she makes you beg like a dog for scraps."

Ignoring the camera and the man lurking behind it, I focus on the two people in front of me. "You got any lube in here, Az?"

"In the bathroom. Top drawer," she pants. "But please don't pull out. I'm so close. Please."

I tug harder on her hair. "Does it feel good, pretty girl? You like me fucking this wet pussy while you ride Cyrus's face?"

"Yes, please don't stop."

The way she begs has me on edge. I want to hear more, so much more. So I pull out.

"No," Azadeh whines. "Zeke, what are you doing? Please."

"In all the years I've known you, Az, I've never heard you ask me for anything. It's shocking how much I enjoy hearing you plead in that whispering tone. You know you're my queen, and I'll always worship you. I'd kneel like a dog for you, the knight ready to die at your command. But hearing you beg does something to me. Something dark and depraved that wants to dominate you until you're on the cusp and can't take anymore."

"Please, Zeke. Please."

I slam into her, holding her hair like a rein and pushing in deep. I need her to know what she does to me and how I come undone for her. "Such a good girl. You feel that, Az? How deep I'm in your perfect little pussy?" I yank her hair until she turns her head. "That's it, Princess. Look at me while I fuck my tight little cunt. You belong to us, Azadeh. Go off and fight, save all those lives, and make the world right. Do what you need to do. But know this, baby girl, your wet little hole will only ever be for us. You belong to us."

Azadeh screams in ecstasy and pain as I bend and bite the delicate flesh of her shoulder, my teeth sinking in like an animal starved for far too long. I'm ravenous. Consumed with desire. All logical thoughts are vanquished, and only desperation remains.

"I'm going to pound in this cunt so hard and cum so deep in you. Maybe I'll put babies in you, Az, to keep you tethered to us. What do you think about that, pretty girl? I'll force you to stay. Tie you to a bed so we can breed you. Load after load of cum until your belly is big with our child. You can justify abandoning us to save the world, but would you be able to deprive your child of your love?"

"Zeke." She says my name like a prayer, a plea that has me unsure if it's from ecstasy or something else.

"The best and worst thing I've ever done was falling in love with you, Princess," I growl, the words hibernating in the part of my heart that's only ever belonged to her. The only girl I've ever been with. The only girl who's ever held my heart. "You're the girl who never wants to stay, no matter what I do. "Divaneh shodam, jāné del-am."

I've gone crazy, the life of my heart.

I whisper the words in Persian, hoping to make it clear. Because that's what Azadeh is for me, and has been from the moment I saw her that day when I was a scared, confused boy. She's always been the spark that lights my heart. My reason for living. Sure, over the years, I've found another type of love with Cyrus and Lev, but without Azadeh, there's always been a missing core. Without her, we're simply bodies walking around without hearts—Tinmen from The Wizard of Oz.

"Why can't you stay?" I grit the words through clenched teeth, my restraint holding on by a fraying thread.

I thrust inside her with force and spit above her ass crack, pushing my saliva down to her puckered asshole. Inserting the tip of my thumb, I press it inside her. Removing my hand from her hair, I shove my fingers into her mouth. I want to invade every single inch of her. To have her full of me, to show her with my actions what she does to my being. "We need you. We desperately need you. When you come home, we're whole. Then you leave, and the darkness takes over, Az. You're our fucking light, don't you see that? Fuck, Lev took Mona because he needed you. He fuckin' *needed* you, and you weren't here."

I tug at her, forcing her neck to turn as her mouth opens further for me. "I've never wanted to debase you, Azadeh. Never wanted to be cruel to you. Even when you admitted to liking degradation, I still refused. I didn't think I should say those words to someone who represents the divine. But right now, I want to hurt you the way you've hurt me. With everything I've gone through, the years of abuse from my father, losing my eye, the years in prison, none of it compared to the pain of waiting around for you."

Chapter 21

Lev Age 30

Darkness shrouds me in the little surveillance room I've set up. My little shelter of deviance. The room that houses my secrets and perversions. I grip my dick as I watch the monitors. Forty screens cover three naked bodies, and the surround sound captures every filthy word and moan uttered in ecstasy.

I thought I was clever, keeping my dirty little secret. Turns out, I wasn't as sly as I thought.

Cyrus winked at me after Zeke's long speech about what a useless piece of shit I was. Okay, he might not have uttered those words, but the gist was pretty much the same. If I'm being honest, he's not wrong. My issues have fucked up my life. Unlike Cyrus and Zeke, who can move on with life, I'm still frozen in place with my mother's hands on my shoulders as I gaze in horror.

Occasionally, I wonder if I enjoy voyeurism because of what my mother forced me to do. Like now, for instance, as I watch three people I love. It should disgust me, but I've long suspected the illness that afflicted my parents is also in my DNA.

You're watching adults, not children.

I know my proclivity isn't the same. Cyrus, Zeke, and Azadeh know I'm lurking behind the monitors. But I still can't ignore that nagging guilt.

My eyes are glued to the monitor. Azadeh's sitting on Cyrus's mouth, making me wish it was my face she was riding.

Zeke pulls at her mouth, forcing her to look at the camera. "Enjoying the show, Peeping Tom?"

Zeke's anger is palpable. I sense his frustration, fear, and rage through the monitor. So much that I wouldn't be surprised if his hand emerged through the screen to strangle me. But the rage he hides so well makes my dick throb.

I spit on my hand and bring it to my shaft. I work my dick, imagining Zeke taking his frustration on me.

"You touching yourself, Levinston?" Zeke asks.

"Yes," I whisper into the safety of the dark room.

He smiles as if he can see me and quickens his thrusts into Azadeh, his thumb deep in her ass. My mouth waters as saliva falls from Azadeh's mouth, sliding down her nipples and falling onto Cyrus's forehead.

Cyrus lifts his hands and twists Azadeh's nipples. He's not gentle. Cyrus has always been better at taking charge of her body. He has no problem hurting her like she wants. Degrading words fall from his lips so easily, and he's the best at sexually gratifying her.

Zeke fulfills her emotionally. He understands her on a level that Cyrus and I never could. Azadeh and Zeke discuss poetry, politics, and religion. They have an intellectual connection. The orgasms they share are heightened but in a different way.

I don't know what I can offer Azadeh besides buying her anything she wants. It might be enough for some women, but not Azadeh. That girl doesn't want what's in my bank account; she longs to possess my soul.

Zeke lifts Azadeh off him and walks away. She seems not to care as her grinding on Cyrus's face intensifies. This woman is so brave and powerful. Even during sex, she has no problem demanding what she wants and taking it.

When I first met Azadeh, I didn't know that a woman could look like her and be kind and strong. My mother was beautiful, but her heart was black, and her strength was non-existent. She had no issue hurting those without power. She was a shell of a woman, and I thought all women were cruel like her. But the moment I met Azadeh, something in her eyes lured me in. As I got to know her, her brave heart and wicked mind made me stay.

"Fuck, baby girl," Zeke groans. "It's hot watching you take what you want. I think before I fuck that tight little pussy again, I'm gonna need you to cum for me. Ride that tongue until you drip into Cyrus's mouth. You know how much he loves cum, baby. Be a good girl and give it to him."

Azadeh grips Cyrus's hair and presses down on his face, grinding until her head falls back, and she moans.

Zeke steps forward and yanks Azadeh's hair until she stands and faces him. "Good girl."

Zeke presses his lips to hers and kisses her with fevered passion, pushing her against the wall. Of all the ways I imagine touching Azadeh, the one I yearn for the most is the sensation of her lips against mine.

Cyrus rises from the floor and grabs the bottle of lube dangling from Zeke's hand. "Get her on the bed. I want her slutty legs up, and that pussy open nice and wide. You're going to be a good boy, Zeke, and fuck my dirty slut until she screams. And I'm going to fuck your ass until you cum deep inside her."

Zeke doesn't stop kissing Azadeh. He places his hands under her ass and lifts her. She wraps her legs around his waist. "I'm gonna fuck this tight little pussy. Fuck you up against the wall. Once this tight cunt is full of my cum, I'm going to put you on the bed and open your legs so Lev can zoom in and watch me leak out of you."

I'm shocked the drywall isn't falling around them as Zeke pounds into her. His thrusts are desperate, like the motion of my hand on my cock. Sex for the four of us has never been about orgasms and gratification. Zeke and Cyrus would've banged their way through life if it were. Azadeh never placed any physical loyalty on us. She's never once demanded fidelity.

But for us, sex is about healing the fractured pieces of our past. Through sex, the three of them have healed. Something I've still not managed to do. No matter how badly I wanted that connection over the years, I've never been able to break the dysfunctional bonds of my past tethered to my fragile brain. The only time I've ever touched her was with the barrel of a gun or while she was drugged into a deep slumber. Fleeting moments that should've been transcendental were abhorrent. When she was asleep, I didn't feel pressure, and when I held the gun, I felt safe.

"Look at me." Zeke's order forces my eyes to him. The command is for Azadeh, but I can't help but obey.

He grabs her jaw, turning her to face him. "Eyes on me while I'm fucking you, Princess. I want those pretty brown eyes knowing exactly whose cock is making you so fucking wet."

Azadeh wraps her arms around his shoulders, her forehead touching his. The scene is so intimate and powerful. I almost avert my gaze, but the intimacy has my cock ready to blow. Sexual acts are a dime a dozen. I could load up my computer with porn and watch a girl who looks like Azadeh getting rammed by fifty different men if I wanted. But what I crave are these moments of intimate truths. Scraps of love I desperately want but don't know how to ask for.

"I'm feeling left out here," Cyrus whines.

Zeke and Azadeh laugh. Humor has always been Cyrus Porter's forte. I've always envied him for that ability. I don a mask of indifference and snobbery to shield myself from the ongoing pain while he uses laughter. My way causes loneliness, and he creates joy.

"What do you think, Princess? Should we let him have a little fun?" Zeke asks Azadeh.

"I'm gonna fuckin' destroy you for that, Ezekiel," Cyrus growls. "Nine inches is about to go up that tight ass, and I'm gonna make it hurt."

Zeke laughs as he carries Azadeh to the large California King bed. "Oh, look at Freddy Kruger over here inflating his numbers. That's eight inches at best."

Cyrus discards the lube and pushes Zeke down on top of Azadeh. "We'll see how big it is when you're begging Daddy to stop hurting your puckered little hole for being a bad boy."

Cyrus falls to his knees and pulls Zeke's ass apart with his large hands before swirling his tongue around his anus.

I close my eyes for a moment as I switch between the desire of wanting to fuck my friends and wanting them to fuck me. My only real sexual experiences have been with Zeke.

He allowed me to tie him up while I explored his body and mine. Having him tied up lessened my anxiety. He assured me he wouldn't accidentally touch me in the heat of passion. And from those sessions, I knew how fuckin' perfect and tight his ass was. How my cock fit so perfectly, and how he moaned with pleasure as I came deep in his asshole. I remember the shock and pleasure in his eye and his deep moans as my tongue probed his ass, licking him clean.

"Mmm," Cyrus moans. "I love eating this fucking ass. One day, Lev will get over his hangups, and we'll run a train on your pretty hole, Zeke. We'll fill it and suck out all the cum we pump inside."

"Jesus, why is that so hot?" Azadeh says as her nails dig deep into Zeke's back.

I watch on the screen as Azadeh leaves a trail of blood on his skin. She always draws blood with knives, nails, or her teeth during sex. Sometimes, she licks the blood; others, she steps back and admires her handy work. This particular proclivity garnered her the affectionate nickname of Little Vampire—a name Cyrus occasionally uses instead of Hellcat.

Cyrus chuckles as he rises from his knees. He grabs the lube, pops the cap, and pours the liquid on his dick and between Zeke's ass cheeks. "You think that's hot, Hellcat? Wait until you see our boy begging for me to fuck his ass until he can't see straight."

Cyrus lines up his dick. Zeke growls as Cyrus forgoes prep and pushes his cock inside him.

"How many inches is it now, baby?"

"Fuck, that stings," Zeke says hoarsely, moaning in pain and pleasure.

Cyrus grabs Zeke's hips and thrusts. "Admit that I'm hung like a motherfuckin' horse, or I'll decimate you."

"Is something in my ass?" Zeke asks Azadeh. "I swear Cyrus said he was going to fuck me, but I can't feel shit. Only mild discomfort of a whiny little bitch talkin' a big game when he has absolutely no follow through." Zeke pushes his ass back. "Still trying to find a dick here. Here dicky, dicky. Come here, boy."

Cyrus growls, holding Zeke down and thrusting repeatedly. "Feel it now, Zeke? Feel how your tight little ass is begging to get fucked? How I'm using it as my cunt? My giant cock will make your pathetic ass its cum dump." He slaps Zeke's ass, leaving a red handprint. "Better fuck our girl. Don't get lazy because your hot little ass got dickmatized by my big cock."

I smile at their banter. So light and easy. Unlike the banter between Cyrus and me, which holds a bit of animosity, Zeke jokes that the sexual tension between us will erupt like a volcano when it finally happens. When I'm ready. But Cyrus won't let me tie him up. I can't blame him. His father tied his hands and feet before burning him. Cyrus will try anything but bondage. It's a limit he can't overcome.

Zeke and Cyrus move faster, their vigorous thrusts becoming a competition. Azadeh is the first to come. Her legs tighten around Zeke's waist as her head falls back, and she screams.

"It's okay, Zeke. Come for Daddy. I know my dick is making you feel good," Cyrus coaxes.

I increase my tempo on my dick to match the rapid movements of Cyrus's hips until he and Zeke grunt out their orgasms. Seeing the three people I love more than anything satiated and satisfied has ropes of cum spewing from my cock all over my hand in frantic waves.

I don't budge from my seat or clean my cum-covered hand. I watch with bated breath as Cyrus pulls out and asks, "Az, you still carry reusable straws in your purse."

"Um, yeah." Azadeh frowns. "That's a random question. There's one attached to my purse. It's by the chaise."

"Don't move, Zeke," Cyrus commands.

Grabbing Azadeh's black leather purse, he removes the stainless-steel tube. Extracting the straw from inside it, he moves behind Zeke and parts his ass with one hand. Bending, he inserts the metal straw in Zeke's ass and closes his mouth over the other end.

Jesus fuckin' Christ, he's sucking the cum out.

Unconsciously, I bring my cum covered hand to my mouth, and my tongue darts out. As Cyrus sucks out Zeke's cum, I lick my fingers and palm clean of my release. Cyrus removes the straw from Zeke's ass but keeps it in his mouth and walks closer to the camera. The surrounding screens suddenly all have creamy liquid obstructing my view.

"Stop acting like a little bitch, Lev. I know you've been watching the whole time."

I see Zeke and Azadeh rising from the bed on a clear area of the screen. Azadeh's back is to me as Zeke takes her in his arms, holding her tight. I wince at the sight of the crisscross scars on her back. I think about the man who put those scars there and what we did to him when we found him living in America.

Chapter 22

Lev - Age 26

Arizona Desert

"**P**lease, let me go. I have a family. A wife. Two young children. They need me." The man pleaded. He'd been begging from the moment I shoved my gun against his temple.

"Did you care when you placed nooses around all those innocent Iranians' necks?" Zeke asked coldly as he tapped two spoons on his knee.

I'd never seen Zeke Kill anyone. Unlike me, he wasn't in the habit of dropping bodies.

"I've killed no one," Ali protested.

But we knew he had. We'd spent hours researching online and looking up cases, and we were sure beyond all doubt that this man was responsible for wielding the whip that scarred Azadeh and so much more.

Zeke grabbed the file and threw it on the ground at Ali's knees. Hundreds of photos slipped out of the vanilla folder. "Fuck you, motherfucker. We know exactly who you are." Zeke picked up a photo of a girl who couldn't have been older than thirteen. In the picture, she was smiling and holding up a peace sign. "You remember her? Shirin Mousavi? She wanted to be a human rights lawyer. You and your buddies raped her before you dragged her to the noose." Zeke grabbed the man by his hair and dragged him a few inches to another photo. "What about him? He tried to help his father as you hanged him. You slapped him so hard that when he fell, he hit his head and died two days later from a brain aneurysm."

Zeke kicked Ali in the face, making the man fall back. Gathering all the photos from the sand, Zeke dropped all but one on Ali's chest. "What about this girl?" He held up a picture of Azadeh at twelve, dressed head to toe in black. The only part of her visible was her sweet face. Zeke stomps on Ali's chest. "You remember this girl? Remember how you whipped while she cried and begged you to stop? Remember how you told her she was a whore for showing an inch of her hair?" Zeke smashed his foot into Ali's face repeatedly until blood pooled on the Arizona sand. "You remember her, Kosketch?"

Kosketch was one of the many Persian swear words I'd learned from Azadeh's brother. The direct translation was a pimp or a cuckold, depending on how you saw it. But Persians used it interchangeably for an asshole or a dishonorable person. Never in all my years of knowing Azadeh had I ever heard her swear in Farsi. I asked her once why she swore so easily in English and not in Persian, and she said, "Persian swear words are far too crass and direct."

Ali squirmed like a pathetic reptile as he tried to wriggle away from Zeke. "Please. I've changed. I'm not the same man."

"That's what my father said when I stood above him like this," Zeke spit. "You see this eye?" Zeke pointed to his eye patch. "My father did this. Despite all the violence he inflicted on me to that point, I didn't lay a hand on him." The sun reflected off the spoon as Zeke held it in the air. "He used a spoon similar to this one." He bent until his face hovered over Ali's. "The only time I harmed my father was when he threatened the girl I loved. When he insulted her and demeaned her, I bashed his head in with my mother's favorite pot. It was the only thing in the vicinity. And when he said he'd kill my whore, well, that's when I showed him what it was like to lose an eye. But I didn't stop there."

"Can we hurry the fuck up?" Cyrus demanded. "It's hotter than a whore in church out here."

"Church," Zeke said as he gazed out. "I've hated that word for most of my life. Can you guess why, Ali?"

"No," Ali said, his voice cracking as he shook his head.

"Because a man like you," Zeke spit, "used religion and its institution to create terror in my heart."

The man was shedding tears. The fucker had killed all those innocent people, and he was crying for his miserable life.

"Why are you scared of death, Ali?" I asked. "Shouldn't you be looking forward to death? Don't you believe that all those you killed deserved it? Weren't all those deaths and violent lashings for God? If you truly believe in God, especially an Abrahamic one, you must know the first thing he demands of his children is not to kill. Wonder where you'll end up, Ali?"

"Please, if you kill me, you're sinning. You'll burn too," Ali cried as he listened to my taunts.

I chuckled as I dug a hole in the sand beside Cyrus. "The thing is, Ali, I'm okay with internal emanation. Hell can't be any worse than the demonic situations I've witnessed."

Cyrus flicks his zippo with one hand and points to his face with the other. "I was born in a fire. Besides, living with flames has a certain poetic appeal to me."

Ali's eyes darted between Zeke, Cyrus, and me, searching for the weakest link. "I don't want to die. Please have mercy."

Zeke scoffed. "All you poser devout Abraham's followers are the same. Cry out for mercy when you have none for anyone. But I'll tell you what, Ali. I'll give you the same treatment your bosses gave Marjan Abedini. She pleaded with them, telling them that the man raped her, but the authorities punished her for adultery. So, I'm going to take an eye because that's biblical, and I like to stay true to my roots. Then, I'm going to give you the same opportunities that you and your friends gave Marjan."

Ali's face morphed into shock as Zeke dipped the tip of the spoon into his eye. Zeke gripped Ali's throat, holding him still as he scooped out his eye with the spoon. Ali's tortured screams drowned out the pop *of his eye leaving its socket. Zeke discarded it on the golden sand.*

I'd never heard anyone cry the way Ali did as he searched the desert sand for his missing eye.

Zeke grabbed Ali's collar and dragged him toward the ditch Cyrus and I had been digging. I smiled at Ali before I kicked his body into the hole, and we covered his body with the dirt, leaving only his head protruding.

"Please don't do this. Please!" Ali screamed in a last desperate effort to save his life.

"Now, now, Al," Cyrus crooned as he pulled two pillowcases full of rocks from the car's trunk. "Pray to God, and if he wills it, you'll free yourself. Once you're free, we'll spare your life. Isn't that how you killed those women? Isn't that the rule?"

"Men are to be buried to the waist," Ali squealed.

My trigger finger itched to blow his brains out, but Zeke was adamant about the method of killing—this man had to die in the same way he'd facilitated the deaths of others. He had to experience humiliation and despair. A bullet was too quick and too merciful.

"Ali," I said, "You think you're a man?"

Ali opened his mouth to respond, but his head jerked back as the first rock caught bounced off his forehead. It was the first of many. Zeke threw one after another. A large one hit his nose, and we heard the bone break. Another oozed blood from his temple.

The three of us were like kids throwing a baseball as we slammed stones into the man.

Soon, Ali's screaming halted, and his head hung to the side, his blood-covered lashes flickering slowly.

Cyrus pulled a rag from his pocket and filled it with a few rocks. He walked to the car trunk and dosed the rag with gasoline before returning to Ali. Yanking his head back, Cyrus pushed the burning cloth into Ali's mouth and laughed as he watched his head burn.

Chapter 23

Azadeh   Age 29
Present Day

"Y ou know Dariyus is going to kill you for not calling him instead of The Cinders, right?" Zeke whispers in my ear as we get off Lev's private plane.

"Briar is having a baby. My brother doesn't need to be worried. We've got this. Besides, Alaric is good at all the espionage stuff and has more connections than Lev."

Zeke laughs. "Don't let Lev hear you say that."

We were briefed in the morning before we piled into the jet. The group holding my sister was called SALT, a religious cult that kidnapped children and young women. They didn't take Mona for their usual reasons. Mona was being leveraged for money. We still didn't understand how they got her since Lev's house is secluded and has a state-of-the-art surveillance system. There was nothing on the monitor to show it was even them who took her.

"Why did you think I was working for The Cinders in the first place? Alaric's connections from the club have come in handy. He's made some strong connections with the black market in Iran. I wanted it. Besides, they're fantastic guys who were in a shitty situation."

Zeke chuckles. "Good guys don't fuck their stepmother and kill all her husbands."

I glare at Zeke. "It's complicated. Trust my judgment, okay? They aren't that bad. Besides, without them, I doubt we'd have a concrete plan. Lev has blueprints, but Alaric has a way in. Apparently, the leader is a frequent patron of the club. Into some funky shit, too. If the man has a cult, why is he bothering to find services that cater to his brand of crazy?"

"The cult is pretty new," Zeke says. "Maybe he's in the good guy stage. Not that I've accumulated enough power to show you all the crazy I'm about."

"We're going to see Markus Issacson," Alaric states. "He's the one in charge of Mona's care." He turns to Lev. "You have the money?"

"Yes," Lev says. "One billion dollars."

My heart drops to my stomach. "One billion dollars? Lev, do you even have that kind of money?"

Alaric laughs. "Levinston is worth one hundred billion dollars. You don't know who his parents were? The Cartwrights were filthy rich. Generational wealth in astronomical amounts."

I've always understood that Lev had money, but apparently, he has God-like amounts of money.

Zeke bends and whispers in my ear, "You were a kept woman and didn't even realize it."

I glare at him. "Pardon me?"

Zeke laughs. "Who do you think paid for you to go off and save all those women?"

If someone punched me in the face right now, it would feel less shocking. "What do you mean? I was working with various organizations. Ex-military and martial arts experts. I worked with humanitarians."

I looked at Lev, standing with one of Alaric's hired guns.

"He paid for it all, Az. He said that if you were going off to do foolish things, he'd ensure you were safe. He gave them all explicit orders to leave you alone unless you were in danger. Their entire purpose was to protect you. He's spent billions over the years." Zeke drapes his arm around me. "I told you, you're his security blanket. He was mostly fine until you went to Iran. That's when he lost his mind and made some unfortunate decisions, like taking Mona."

"I wish he'd shown Mona his face. She might not have run off if Lev had told her it was him the whole time. I have no idea why he didn't."

Zeke kisses my cheek and pulls me close. "Love makes people blind, deaf, dumb, and stupid. He couldn't see anything other than you. He regrets his choices. You probably won't be able to forgive him, but you should. His broken pieces are a little more complicated. Besides, he didn't have you to help him like I did. Not when he was young, scared, and alone."

Lev stands straight as he speaks with Alaric. He's focused, and I know that deep down, he's kicking himself for what he's done. If we get

Mona back safe and sound, I won't hold it against him. As much as a part of me wants to make him beg and wallow, a bigger part of me loves him too much to deny him. I'll find other ways to punish him, but refusing him my love will not be part of the equation. I won't break his spirit like his mother did.

A black limo pulls up to the hangar.

"Everyone ready?" Alaric asks.

"Let's do this." Cyrus beams. He's always ready for anything that entails a fight. If The Purge was an actual event, Cyrus would do a year-long countdown in anticipation of the big day. I should be worried about how much he likes carnage.

The limo pulls up to an abandoned warehouse. It looks like an area that was booming at one time, but all that remains is abandoned warehouses and industrial plants.

I survey the area as we exit the limo to see if there's any way they can infiltrate us. I can't see any people, and only one car is in the parking lot.

Zeke startles me as he grabs my hand, his fingers squeezing. "It's gonna be all right. I won't let anything happen to you or Mona."

"No." I shake my head. "*I* won't let anything happen to Mona or me."

He smiles, but it doesn't reach his eye like usual. "You know it's not sexist for a man who loves you to want to take care of you, right? It's not like I'm asking you to be barefoot and pregnant in the kitchen."

We all approach the decrepit cement stairs leading to a steel door. Alaric tugs the metal handle, and the door opens. A simple tug. No security, no codes.

I shiver as the stench of vomit and piss assaults me. Fear clutches at my throat, making it hard to breathe. "This is where they've kept my sister?"

As the words leave my lips, I see all the blood. I don't want to pay these men and go on my merry way. I want them to suffer. Mona is privileged to pay to get out of this circumstance, but what about the other girls these monsters abduct?

I squeeze Zeke's hand, and he lowers his ear to my mouth. "He has to die."

I don't know when I decided that death is an acceptable outcome for certain people. It sure wasn't from my mother, who firmly believed in tolerance. Even with all she went through, Nasrin Baran demonstrated the virtue of mercy.

But I don't.

Forgiveness isn't possible for those who have no issue harming others. Men who rape, steal, torture, and kill can't change. All they can do is fake it until they're convinced they have society fooled. Men who use religion as a tool for corruption cannot be allowed to obtain power. Divinity becomes a weapon in their arsenal, powerful enough to brainwash the masses.

Alaric halts at a large door. Two men with semi-automatics strapped to their backs talk into a walkie-talkie before opening the doors.

"Alaric," says a thin man with a goatee and greasy hair. He stands from his chair and raises his hand for Alaric to shake.

"Not sure if pleasantries are warranted, Marcus," Alaric sneers, refusing to shake the man's hand. "You kidnapped someone important to me. I'm sure you realize that this altercation means the end of any business deals my organization has with yours."

Marcus laughs. "Dear Alaric, with the money I'll be gaining today, I could buy your organization ten times over."

"Let's cut the bullshit," Lev says as he opens the briefcase.

"That's not the amount we agreed on," Marcus says in disgust. "Where is the rest of it? This is a quarter of a million at most."

"No suitcase in the world could house that amount of paper bills," Lev states. "We have your Cayman account, and we'll wire the rest of the money once the girl is returned to us safely."

"Levinston Cartwright, I assume?" Marcus asks. "Your parents threw wonderful events with the best party favors. Such a shame you didn't continue their legacy."

Lev's back stiffens, and his eyes go blank. That same look he gets when he's touched. I want to jump in front of him and stab Marcus until his body goes limp and falls on the floor at Lev's feet.

Lev looks away from Marcus and shuts the briefcase, regaining his composure. "Yes, well, my parents' interests and mine differ drastically. Now, I suggest we forgo discussions about the past and continue with our negotiations."

Marcus laughs and pulls out his phone. "Bring the girl in."

A large man bursts through the door with my sister. She looks good and has no visible markings. Her eyes are alert, and her hair and clothes are clean.

I free myself from Zeke and run to her, wrapping my arms around her tight. "Joonam."

Tears fall from Mona's eyes as she returns my hug. She keeps saying sorry in Persian. *Mote'as-sefam.*

"Shh. I've got you. There's nothing to be sorry about. I've got you."

"As you can see," Marcus says, "the girl is fine. So how about you wire that money, and we can all be on our way?"

I wrap my arm around Mona's shoulder and hand her to Zeke. Pulling my knife, I turn and throw it across the room. The blade lands in Marcus's throat.

The big dude pulls a gun, but Lev is quicker and puts a bullet between the man's eyes, causing blood and brain matter to splatter Cyrus's black hoodie.

Cyrus shrugs. "It's cool. Everything washes out of black."

The two guards barge in, but before they can do anything, Cyrus has one in a chokehold while Zeke has the other pinned against the wall, his gun at his head.

"Looks like this turned into a party after all," Cyrus says as he pulls out his zippo. The guy screams as Cyrus holds a flickering flame against his face, and his flesh burns. "Azadeh, what do you think about me starting a perfume business? There has to be a market for Eau de Burned Flesh." He bends and sniffs the man's cheeks. "Even this piece of shit now smells divine."

My gaze moves from Cyrus to Zeke. He has a spoon held upright under the man's eye. Shock takes over as I witness how ruthless my sweet Zeke can be. I always grasped that Cyrus was a bit unhinged, but seeing Zeke push a spoon into someone's flesh and scoop an eye out so effortlessly is a little jarring. Never in a million years did I think him capable of such brutality. The man has a hard time calling me a slut, and here he is, consumed with violence and gore.

The room fills with the screams of the tortured men, so I barely hear Alaric.

"Azadeh, get them under control," Alaric says as he places a small device on the table. "We gotta get out of here. In five minutes, the place will blow. We gotta go."

My gaze flits between Zeke and Cyrus, unsure how I can calm their blood lust. While I'm trying to figure it out, Lev solves the problem by putting a bullet between each guard's eyes.

"Dirty pool, Lev," Cyrus growls. "I was having a good time."

"We gotta go," Lev states.

The six of us sprint out of the building and make it to the limo as the thunderous roar of the explosion echoes behind us and searing heat licks at our backs, leaving us breathless and shaken but alive.

"I'm still bitter. I can't smell the flesh," Cyrus whines. "You owe me a burning carcass, Lev."

I ignore everyone and everything except my sister as we pile into the limo. "You okay?"

"I am now." She moves closer and whispers, "Did you know Zeke was so lethal?"

I shake my head. "No."

"I had such a crush on him. I assumed you were stupid for years because you said he was your friend and not your boyfriend," Mona said, her mouth tipping up in a small smile. "But I feel you, sis. Why settle for one when you can have three? Bet you feel safe knowing they'd all kill for you. I sure do."

I belly laughed, and the men in the limo turned to look at me.

Cyrus cocks an eyebrow. "Care to share the joke with the class?"

I grin. "I was thinking that you're all crazy, but I love you."

"Whoa, you better not be loving this guy over here," Cyrus says, pointing to Alaric. "My self-esteem can't handle another pretty boy. Lev is already too much."

"I'm happily taken," Alaric interjects.

"I think three is more than I can handle," I say as I hug my sister.

"Will you stay?" Mona asks, gazing up at me. "I'd like to have my sister around for more than a few weeks at a time."

"If she had, you wouldn't have been in this mess," Lev mumbles.

I turn to him and glare. "I think you mean if *you* hadn't taken her."

"Wait, Lev was the one who originally kidnapped me?" Mona asks in shock. "Dude, I thought you were the smart one. Why didn't you tell me? I would've played along. Now she's gonna make you beg like a puppy until she forgives you."

Lev shrugs, a sly smile on his lips. "I'd beg your sister until the end of time if it meant she'd be by my side."

Mona glances at me. "Okay, that's some Romeo and Juliet shit. How the heck are you the one with all the luck? I'm lucky if a boy looks at me."

I laugh and hug her closer. "You sure you're okay? They didn't do anything to you?"

"I'm fine," Mona says firmly. "Other than shitty food and a disgusting toilet, nothing happened. But do you think I could take martial arts classes?"

"Oh, yes," I say as relief floods me. "I'll get you trained by the best."

Chapter 24

Cyrus Age 30
Present Day

"So, are we gonna fuck or not?" I ask. "Because I'm getting jealous of soap suds over here."

Azadeh laughs as she glides the loofah along her skin. It's been weeks since she's fucked any of us. Mona was home, and all she wanted to do was spend time with her sister. I love Mona, but that girl is a grade-A cock blocker. She also didn't want Zeke and me to fuck. I'm not sure what me getting ass with Zeke has to do with Mona, but she point-blank told me the only place I could bust a nut is in my shower. When I tried to argue that Zeke and I could move to the other side of the manor, she said no. I would've broken her rules, but Zeke, the fucking goody-goody, can't tell a small white lie.

Then again, why would Zeke put up a fight when she said he could still work on Lev's issues? That meant he was getting banged because Lev's issues were all about his aversion to physical touch.

"Listen, Az, it's been twenty days. *Twenty*." I flex my forearms. "My right one is substantially bigger than my left. It's your fault that I'm lopsided."

She opens the glass shower door and pokes her head out. "No one forced you to masturbate so much."

I growl. "I had no choice. You made me choose between my dick and balls falling off or my right arm looking like The Hulk, while the left one became Bruce Banner."

She shrugs before turning her face to the cascading waterfall from overhead. "Well, Mona is back at school, so you're welcome to fucking Zeke again."

Oh, the little brat. I slide open the glass door and jump into the shower with her. Azadeh yelps as my hand circles her throat, and I slam her against the wall. "You know what happens to an animal when you starve it too long?"

213

I crush my lips to hers and kiss her passionately. Her lips open for me, and our tongues tangle with desperation. I want her to comprehend how much I need her, not only sexually but in every single way. "You know how insane it is to want to consume someone. I now comprehend the unhinged passion of those crazy men in those dark romance books you used to read. The ones that literally eat the flesh of women they love. Fuckin' psychos, I want to fill myself with you. The hold you have over me has driven me mad."

Azadeh smiles as the tips of her nails dig against the cotton of my shirt, desperate to get to my skin. "Do you want to consume me, Cyrus? Bite into my flesh so we are one. A communion of sorts."

I groan into her neck. How the fuck can someone be so sweet and so insane at the same time. The girl pushes me to the brink of madness and shelters me all at the same time. Azadeh is the sun, and we are planets turning in her orbit.

Azadeh grips my shirt and tears it apart, exposing my bare chest. Her head dips, and she places gentle kisses along my burned-up flesh.

I'm in awe of how easily she worships the ugliest parts of me. There's no hesitation, no moment of disgust; for her, those brutal burn marks are as beautiful as a rose in full bloom. Every time she doesn't see a beast on my flesh, I'm taken aback. Perhaps her inherent ability to look past what others ran from is what drew us all to Azadeh. She saw the men we longed to be and not how the world perceived us.

Azadeh brings forth our goodness and light and banishes the darkness that burrows in our hearts.

"My love for you isn't a drop in the ocean," I whisper in her ear, shocked at how much I mean it. "It's the whole damn universe."

Azadeh's breathing speeds up as her fingers fumble with my belt. She struggles under the stream of water as she pulls the belt off and lowers my soaked jeans to the middle of my thighs. Azadeh grips my erect cock and lines it up to her entrance. "If you mean that, then fuck me like an animal. Don't hold back, don't be gentle. Just make me forget everything except the brutality of your love."

My fingers intertwine with hers as I pull my belt from her hand. "You want me to fuck you like you mean nothing, don't you? Need me to fuck you the way Zeke and Lev never could. You want me to make you feel worthless, used, disposable. Don't you?"

"Yes," she whispers.

"Why," I ask. "Why do you make me degrade you?'

"Because you're the only one who grasps the relief that comes with humiliation. You understand how degradation makes life's burdens and hardships weightless. You respect me as an equal and not as an untouchable. This is what you give me that no one else can."

Azadeh gazes up at me. The water streams through her thick raven hair and frames her beautiful face. A droplet of water falls from her inky eyelashes and lands on her round cheek as I slide the leather behind her delicate neck.

Azadeh beams at me as I secure the belt with the buckle. I place two fingers between the leather and her skin, ensuring it's not so tight that I could accidentally cut off circulation during play. We have our signs—her safe word, Azadi, the word freedom in Farsi, or the two taps on any part of my body or nearby surface.

I grip the belt and yank it forward as my fingers dip down her body and part her lips. Azadeh's legs open, and she shivers as the tip of my index finger flirts with her sensitive clit. "That's it, Hellcat. Open those legs, and let me know what a little slut you are." I tug the belt, forcing Azadeh to her knees. I fist my dick and aim it at her pretty mouth. "I don't think you deserve to feel good. You've been a bad fucking whore by keeping your filthy fuck holes away from me. You're gonna have to earn your orgasms, slut." I slap her face, the tip of my cock pointing above her eyebrows. I drag my dick down until it's directly in front of her lips. "Open up. Put your worthless mouth to good use. Show me why we should keep you around, slut."

Azadeh covers my cock and swallows me whole. My hand hits the wall at the mind-blowing way she's sucking my dick. I have to rein myself in so I don't lose my shit and blow in her hot mouth before we even get started. Her dark eyes gaze up at me as she hollows her cheeks. Her head hits the wall as I thrust, and her ragged gagging drowns out the rainfall from the showerhead.

"Well, what do we have here?"

I turn to see Zeke leaning against the door-frame. He's so fuckin' good looking, even with that pirate eyepatch, his visible eye a sapphire lure that calls to my soul. Fuck, how are these people turning me into a poetic sap?

"Well, when two people like each other, some-times it makes their private parts tingle," I explain as if talking to a five-year-old. "Azadeh is elevating the accumulation of cum in my balls."

"Why don't you come out here, and we can make it a real celebration?" Zeke asks.

"Oh no, Bro. I'm not sharing," I say, glaring at Zeke, annoyed at the interruption. "Besides, you've been having fun with Lev. Now the two of you go off and do whatever weird shit you do while I make my girl choke on cum."

Zeke bends, grabs a metal chain, and yanks it. My eyes widen in shock as Lev stumbles head-first into the bathroom. "You interested now?"

Was I interested? My eyes moved from Azadeh gagged on my dick to Lev on his hands and knees like a dog. I always assumed Lev had a thing for degradation. But when I noticed Azadeh staring at him with lust, I knew there was only one option. A fucking orgy. Full-blown balls to the walls.

I rub the top of Azadeh's hair, bringing her gaze back to me. "You wanna go play with the other little puppy?"

She nods.

I grip her head and hold her fastened to the wall as I bang into her mouth. "I think he'd enjoy you sharing your little treat. Visiting empty-handed is awfully rude, after all."

Chapter 25

Lev Age 30

The brain is a fragile organ that holds our existence at a standstill yet possesses the ability to push our lives forward. It can forge fortresses to protect us and break into a million fragmented pieces when something harms us. The complexities of the brain and the defense mechanisms it creates are something I've lived with since the tender age of four. I've allowed myself brief moments of joy because submerging myself into the tremendous bounty of life opens me up to the ruthless truth that anything worthy also carries the earth-shattering weight of devastation.

Over the years, I yearned to break free and to give and receive love, but my traumatic child-hood blocked that path at every turn. If it hadn't been for Zeke, I'd never know the warmth of human touch. That man has stood by me time and again when I've given him every reason to walk away. I gaze up at him with pure love in my heart for staying by my side and for his patience, understanding, and compassion. I always thought Azadeh was the glue that held us all together. Her love bonded us, but it was Zeke who healed us and, in doing so, himself.

When we returned from the compound, I pulled him aside and told him he needed to push me. I wanted a life, something I'd deprived myself of for so long. I passed him a rope and told him to bind me.

The first session was hard. I screamed with every touch and recalled untold horrors with every brush of his lips against my skin. But I fought through it. I told myself that this was Zeke. He loved me, and I loved him. By being thrown off a cliff, I moved past the first hurdle.

The two of us made discoveries. The first was that I did not like to dominate, and the second was that I was far more comfortable being used. Turns out I'm a submissive. Zeke said it made sense since I was such a control freak, but I was taken aback by it. But when Zeke told me what to do and took my options away, I felt my body relax. For Zeke, it was a triumph because it proved that my body instinctively trusted him, and now that the barrier of my mind had been broken, the obstacles weren't a blatant issue any longer.

So Zeke strapped a collar on me and dragged me to Azadeh's bedroom—the final test.

My gaze locks with Azadeh as she chokes on Cyrus' penis. She's enthusiastic, and he's forceful. All I can think about is how I wish I were between her lips and in her place. Zeke was a gentle top in comparison to Cyrus's brutality. Yet I wanted to know what it would be like to be controlled by Cy. I longed to be the object of his cruelty.

Zeke lights a smoke as he leans against the door frame, appreciating the show in the shower. The thick outline of his dick raged against the cotton of his gray sweatpants. His hand grips my leash as he twists the chain before tugging me forward until my face is directly on his feet. "You think you can do what she's doing, pup?"

My cock throbs at the nickname. Simultaneously degrading and affectionate.

I nod my head.

He laughs as his bare foot nudges my face. His big toe slides along my bottom lip. "Be a good boy and kiss your master's feet." I gaze up at Zeke as my lips pucker, and I place a kiss on the pad of his toe. "Good boy."

I feel ten feet tall as he praises me. The adoration is welcome and desperately wanted.

Zeke tugs at the leash, forcing my body to move upright. I remain on my knees, and we look at the scene before us. Azadeh has one hand on Cyrus's shaft, pumping up and down with the rhythm of her mouth. Her other hand grips his ass, her nails penetrating his skin. My gaze roams Cyrus's body. Half his frame is a black work of art with grooves and dents. What would it be like to lick those scars? What would they taste like?

"Take out my cock," Zeke demands.

My back straightens, and I fumble with the elastic waistband of his pants before pulling them down. His dick springs forward, and my stomach flips with excitement. Zeke's dick is perfect. Smooth, with delicate veins decorating his shaft, The perfect crown with a drop of pre cum pooled on the surface. I lean forward and lick the drop, relishing the salty flavor.

Zeke affectionately rubs the top of my head as a puff of smoke shrouds me. Since he discovered that the act of smoking aroused both of us, he ensures he lights one before we partake in sexual activities.

Zeke's hand moves to the back of my head. He fists a handful of my hair and yanks me back. He smiles down at me as he brings the filter of his cigarette to my lips. My mouth opens and I inhale, holding it in. Zeke brushes the tip of his dick to my mouth, spreading the pre-cum on my lips. A cloud of smoke engulfs his cock as I part for him. Zeke holds my head down, my nose brushing his skin. "That's a good boy. Suck on that cock until you get your treat."

I press my head against Zeke's hand, moving at the speed I know takes him over the edge. The suction of my mouth and flick of my tongue create a masterpiece—a sexual Sonata-allegro. Every moan and groan Zeke utters is the standing ovation for my oral symphony.

"Fuck," Zeke hisses as his hips move, desperate to reach his finale.

"That's it, my pretty little whore, take it all," Cyrus groans.

I tilt my head to the side as his body stiffens, his weight crushing Azadeh to the wall.

My view is quickly obstructed as Zeke grabs the sides of my head and forces me to the task at hand. "Don't make me angry, Pup. You know how much I like good boys."

I want to make Zeke proud of me. To tell me how much of a good boy I am and how proud of me he is. I tune out the temptations and distractions around me and focus on giving the best blow job in all eternity. I want him to come deep down my throat and know that no one will satisfy him like I can.

Zeke brushes the tears that escape my eyes. He holds the wetness and the pad of his thumb before bringing it to his lips and sucking it clean. "I gotta fuck this pretty mouth. I want to hear how much my baby boy cries for daddy when he's being choked."

Zeke's degrading words encourage me and ignite my desire to prove my worthiness. I grab his ass and slide my finger between his cheeks. A low moan escapes Zeke's lips as I press the tip of my index finger against his puckered asshole. I slip it inside slowly, and Zeke slaps the door frame. A jolt of satisfaction goes through me as Zeke comes undone before me. I open my mouth to him and gag as he thrusts in me. My cock aches for relief as I work my hand over his shaft and swirl my tongue around his tip.

"Fuck, baby boy," Zeke says, his voice a mixture of a purr and a growl. "That's it, baby,, take that cock all the way. Good boys know how to deepthroat, don't they?" I gaze up as he places the cigarette filter between his fingers. The smoke creates a messed-up halo around his head. He grips my head as he thrusts his cock to the back of my throat, and for a moment, I'm concerned I might vomit all over him. "You better not puke, Pup, or I'll force you to lick it all up."

I relax my throat, welcoming Zeke's invasion. I want this to be the best blow job he's ever received. I want to make him proud of me.

Zeke's body spasms, and his hot cum coats my tongue and the back of my throat. "Don't swallow, baby boy." He pulls out of my mouth, his dick covered in my saliva and his cum. "You did a good job, baby. I'm proud of you."

I turn to stare at Azadeh. Her position mirrors mine, both of us on our knees on a leash, mine with links and hers made of leather.

"Fuck," Cyrus grunts. "Open your mouths. Show us the cum." Azadeh and I open our lips, displaying the cum in our mouths. "Kiss. Swap that cum. Show us how dirty our whores are. But don't you swallow a drop."

Chapter 26

The hunger and fear in Lev's eyes have my stomach rolling and my heart racing. I want to see what he'll do. Will he take charge, or will he need me to push him until he breaks? The last time shocked me when he took the barrel of his gun and put it inside me. It was a side of Lev I'd never seen, and it turned me on. But unlike Cyrus and Zeke, it made me want to get the better of him.

Lev leans toward me, and I can almost hear time ticking with anticipation and excruciating slowness.

"You can do it, Pup," Zeke encourages in a whispered hush. I can hear the hope and fear laced in his voice.

Many emotions are present in Lev's luminous gray eyes as they lock with mine. Apprehension, excitement, fear, lust, and even love. I know he's searching within himself for the courage to do this. Exploring the sensation of touch with Zeke is one thing, but Cyrus and I are a whole new ball game.

Zeke steps forward and pets the top of Lev's head. "Go on, Pup. You're doing such a good job. I'm very proud of you."

Lev nods and molds his hand to my nape. His touch singes my skin as he pulls me forward and tentatively brushes his lips to mine. My eyes flutter before closing, and I fall into the kiss. Ten years of craving this man and never being able to have him crash around me. I'm lost in the moment. Emotions collide, and I'm unsure what I feel from one second to the next— passion, need, desperation, desire, and, most of all, love.

I grip his head as droplets of water fall from my hair onto the marble floor below us. My fingers pull at the chestnut strands, yanking him closer. Our tongues dance as we push our spit and the guys' cum back and forth. A frenzied need builds between us, limbs tangled as we finally experience the desire we've wanted for so long.

"That's it, Pup," Zeke whispers. "Show her how badly you want her. Let her see what a good boy you are."

I look at Zeke as I push the cum back and forth from my mouth to Lev's. Cyrus is standing behind him, his hand on Zeke's thick shaft, pumping his cock, thickening it. I want him to fuck me. I want them all to fuck me. I want to be full of them as they grab me and they rip me apart before putting me back together.

"Give Azadeh all the cum, Pup," Zeke orders.

Lev grips my head and leans me back before pouring the fluids from his mouth into mine. He pulls away, breathing heavy, eyes hooded. "I loved you the moment I saw you. Scared and helpless, discarded and traumatized. The only emotion I knew was fear, and the only vision I saw was terror. Until you. You appeared, and it was like you hit me with a spell. I'm sorry it's taken me this long to touch you and be touched by you. Thank you for never turning your back on me, even when I deserved it."

His words grab my heart in their grip and squeeze. I place my hands on his face and nod. I want to tell him how much I love him, how I'll always be there for him and always have his back, but the cum and spit in my mouth make that impossible. So I nod and hope he knows every thought and emotion fluttering in my mind.

Cyrus pulls Lev off me by his neck. "Good job, little whore."

I glare at Cyrus as he calls Lev a whore. I'm unsure if he's ready for the dominance that Cyrus loves. I've learned over the years that I enjoy degradation. I never thought I would, but I do. There's something powerful about words from someone you know will keep you safe and love you. I've reclaimed those degrading words. They can no longer harm me. Whore is no longer spat at me to shame me for being liberated or condemn me for not wanting to live by their puritanical religious rule. I'm no longer the ten-year-old bullied by a fifty-year-old man because I tapped my foot to a popular song or manhandled by the police and whipped for showing an inch of hair. When Cyrus degrades me, I hold the power. I possess the control. He only goes as far as I let him, and he won't hurt me if I demand it to stop.

Cyrus slaps Lev's face with his cock. "What's your safe word, cum dump?"

Lev gazes up at him and whispers, "Red."

"Oh, you went with a classic," Cyrus grunts as he slides the tip of his dick along Lev's lips. "Azadeh's is Azadi. Zeke's is church, and mine is peace. Be a good little cum rag, and make sure you remember that." Lev opens his mouth, and Cyrus thrusts his hips until his dick is nestled inside. "Damn, Lev, who knew you'd be a world-class cock whore?"

"You enjoying the show, Princess?" Zeke asks as he yanks my head to look at him.

I nod, still unable to speak.

Zeke chuckles. "I want everything you're holding in that pretty little mouth. Every single drop, baby." He presses his lips to mine, parting my lips with the tip of his hot tongue before swiping it inside to collect everything from my mouth.

He leaves me on the floor as he walks to Cyrus. Cy smiles as he pulls Zeke toward him by the nape of his neck. They kiss, and the visual is stimulating. Zeke's hand moves to Lev's head as he pushes him further onto Cyrus's dick, holding him there forcefully.

My gaze moves from Zeke's hand to his face, and I watch him and Cyrus kiss passionately. These two have always been fire together. Cyrus does something for Zeke that Lev and I can't.

I never thought I could be in a nontraditional relationship. I always wanted the husband and two kids running around the yard. Never in a million years did I think I'd be in a polyamorous relationship. I always assumed I'd want my spouse to be loyal to me sexually and never look at anyone else. But love is like water. Your body can never have enough of it, and the more you drink, the healthier you will be. I know society might always side-eye what the four of us have, but the truth is that society is rarely right in its opinions. All I know is I'm happy. My men are happy, and that's enough for me. Because at the end of the day, all anyone wants is to feel joy, no matter how that joy might appear.

I watch as Zeke tips Cyrus's head back, and the cum and saliva spill from his mouth into Cy's.

"You know what to do," Zeke whispers before turning to Lev. "Look up at Cy, Pup. You've been a good boy and deserve a treat." Lev glances up as Zeke steps back. "Keep your mouth open, nice and wide for Cyrus, Pup."

Lev listens obediently, his mouth gaping wide. His eyes are on Cyrus as he transfers the cum and spit into his mouth.

"Drink it up like a good little fuck boy," Cyrus demands, and Lev complies.

"Princess," Zeke says, turning to me. "I'm gonna need you to go get on your bed, spread those legs nice and wide so we've got a clear view of that sexy pussy."

I hear Zeke laughing as I hop up, run from the bathroom, and jump on my bed like a kid excited about birthday presents and cake.

Zeke picks up the metal chain from the bathroom floor and tugs it, stepping out of the bathroom with Lev crawling behind him.

"If I'd known I could make this bitch submit like a good little puppy, I would have gotten him a collar and leash years ago," Cyrus says, walking behind. He stops dead in his tracks as his eyes shift from Lev to me, spread eagle on the bed, before he quickly runs out of the bedroom.

Zeke and I look at each other in confusion as we hear Cyrus's footsteps echoing in the upstairs hall and down the stairs.

Zeke shrugs as he grabs the remote from the dresser and turns on the wall-mounted television above my head.

An image of me sleeping pops up on the screen. The blankets are a mess around me. I'm naked, aside from a t-shirt pulled up below my breasts. My legs are slightly parted.

Lev moves toward the screen, but Zeke yanks his leash, and he stumbles back. I gaze at Lev on the floor, seeing the fear and panic in his eyes. I'm unsure what the big deal is since I know Lev has cameras in all the rooms. And then I see it.

Lev is crouched over my bed, his head between my legs, eating me out as I sleep. I should be mad, but I'm turned the fuck on. It's incredibly exciting to see how desperate Lev is for me. How his head moves rapidly as he licks between my legs. His greed as he drowns in me and only me.

"Our little pup here has hundreds of these videos," Zeke says. "I figured you should see it and dole out a proper punishment." He grabs a magazine from my dresser, rolls it up, and taps Lev on the nose. "You've been a bad boy, haven't you, Pup? You need to be punished, don't you?"

I smile, moving to the edge of the bed. My legs remain open, and I glance at Lev. "Eyes on me, Lev."

Lev looks at me. His gaze roams from my feet to the apex of my thighs to my breasts until they land on my face. "Are you man enough to show me in the light what you did in the shadows? Be a good boy and crawl to me."

Lev moves his hands and knees along the floor until he's facing my center. "You like licking my pussy, don't you?"

He nods slowly.

I grip his chin, placing pressure on his flesh as I ask my question again, this time more forcefully. "I want to hear you say it. What were you doing in those videos?"

Lev's eyes flash with something akin to passion or anger, perhaps a bit of both. "I licked your pussy while you were asleep."

I push his head down so it hovers close to my clit. "Do you want to lick my pussy now? Is our little Pup salivating for a little taste?"

"Yes," Lev whispers, his hot breath on the most delicate part of my flesh.

I caress his head, my fingers dancing in the softness of his hair before I shove his face into my pussy. "Show me Lev. Show me how much you like to lick my pussy. Be a good boy and lick me until I come all over your face. Show me the dirty things you want to do to me in the daylight instead of hiding in the dark."

Lev growls as his nose moves up my slit, and his lips press against my clit, placing a kiss there. He isn't in a rush as his tongue protrudes, and he licks me slowly, working his way along my flesh in a teasing rhythm.

Lev pushes a finger inside me before joining it with two more. Three fingers pump, stretching me as his tongue focuses on my clit. He sucks me into his mouth, his teeth gentle against my flesh.

"That's it, Lev. You're such a good boy," I pant as my toes curl. I want to hold back and prolong the pleasure, but his skill is so phenomenal that

I am not sure I can resist for much longer. "You're so good at this, Lev. You make me feel amazing. Do a good job, and I'll let you lick my pussy all night. Bet you'd like that, wouldn't you? To sleep between my legs and have a little snack every time you wake up, my little pussy licking slut." My words incite Lev. It's as if he's desperate to prove that no one can pleasure me with his mouth like he can. "That's it, baby boy. Show me how much you love to eat my pussy. Yes, use your tongue. You're so good at this. I'm going to come. I'm going to give my good boy a wet treat."

Please," Lev begs. "Please come on my face. Drench me. Please, Azadeh. I'll be such a good boy. Anytime you want this pussy cleaned, I'll do it. I'll suck out all the cum. Use my tongue like toilet paper. I'll do anything to worship this pretty pink cunt."

I hold Lev's head as I wrap my legs around his shoulders and hump his mouth. My breathing speeds up, and my eyes shut as I'm taken to paradise. "I'm going to come, Lev."

"Please drench me," he whimpers as he replaces his fingers with his mouth and drinks my orgasm.

"Fuck, I miss all the good stuff," Cyrus says, standing by the door holding a saffron rock candy stick.

He walks over to Lev and yanks his head back by his hair. Cyrus dips the candy inside me a few times before pulling it out. He winks at me before sucking the candy and pulling it out with a pop. "Fuck, I didn't think it was possible to make this shit sweeter."

Cyrus gazes at Lev, whose face is soaked with my juices. Cy smiles as he rolls the yellow candy along Lev's face. "You're gonna be the best little fuck boy slut, Lev. I can't wait to fucking cum in your tight little ass. Bet you'll lick up your ass cum when it drips onto the floor, won't you? I always knew you'd be at the bottom. A good little subby, ready to do anything your masters demand."

Lev purrs at Cyrus's taunts, relishing the humiliating and degrading words.

"Az, remember when Lev fucked you with his gun?" Cyrus asks.

"Yes," I whisper.

Cyrus smiles. "I think now is as good a time as any to fulfill the promise you made that day."

Chapter 27

Zeke   Age 29

Present Day

I've always loved watching Azadeh in control. The way she moves is poetic, wielding a sexual power that's frightening and artistic. But seeing her behind Lev with her pistol aimed at his ass is the fucking sexist I've ever seen her.

Azadeh's hand is on Lev's lower back, his dick dangling as she pulls apart his cheeks.

Cyrus smirks like a Cheshire cat, the saffron rock candy in his mouth as he pours lube on the barrel of the gun. "Will this ruin the gun? That hunk of metal is expensive as fuck. It's like over four million for the pair or some shit." Cyrus turns to Lev. "That's what you bid, right, fuck boy?"

"Yes," Lev says.

Cyrus grips Lev's face and spits on him. "You address me as sir, slut. The next time you disrespect me, I'm gonna have to fuck that tight little ass with my fist to make sure you understand. Got it, fuck boy?"

Lev's dick jerks, and he visibly shivers at Cyrus's words. Lev blooms under degradation. There's no denying it with the way his body reacts. It took a long time to get here with Lev, and I'm so proud of his growth, how he's allowed people in, and his strength and control.

"He's been prepped," I say as Azadeh grabs the lube. "Be a good boy, Lev, and take the butt plug out of your ass."

Lev reaches behind him and spreads his ass cheeks, displaying the black silicone butt plug.

"Tell them how you've been wearing all day, baby boy. How you love getting your tight asshole stretched nice and wide," I demand.

"Zeke made me walk around all morning with the plug," Lev says. "He fucked me and then plugged up his cum. He's been filling me with cum for the last week."

"Jesus," Cyrus says as he eyes Lev's anus. "That's sick and twisted." Cy looks at me, his lip curling up. "You are a dick-twisted fuck."

Azadeh grips the end of the plug and dislodges the silicone from Lev's asshole before handing it to Cyrus. She slowly points the barrel of the gun at Lev's ass. "You want this in your ass, Lev?'

"Yes," Lev pants.

Azadeh glides the gun between Lev's crack. "Remember when you fucked me with the gun, and I told you one day you beg me to do the same?"

Lev nods. "Yes."

Az smiles. "Start begging, Pup."

"Please, please fuck me with the gun," Lev whimpers.

Azadeh slowly inserts the tip of the metal into Lev's ass. "I think you can do better than that, Lev. You said you wanted to tear me apart. Fuck me like an animal. I don't see any of that now. Where did that bravado disappear to? Did you mean what you said, Lev? Did you want to watch me bleed? Did you want to mark me? Was that a fabrication, an illusion to hide what you wanted the whole time? For me to fuck you. To make you bleed, to break you until you finally cry those tears you've been holding locked in a cage your whole life."

Azadeh's words cut with empathetic brutality. They are honest and direct. Two things Lev needs. It makes sense that Lev is drawn to her because she sees him. She understands things about Lev that Cyrus and I never could.

Azadeh pushes the gun in further, the metal now in Lev's ass to the hilt. "Answer me, Lev."

"Yes. I want to be used. I want to be used by you. By all of you!" Lev screams. His words are drenched with emotion. Each word contains fragments of his struggle. "I want to bleed for you, all of you. I'll be a floor for you to walk on. Take away my need for control. I'm tired of never experiencing the touch of love, and I'm confused about why that touch needs to be rooted in pain, humiliation, and servitude."

Azadeh moves the gun in and out of him, increasing her speed. My cock aches as I witness her power. How she owns it and doesn't care what anyone thinks. My hand moves to where her name is carved on my chest. Jagged lines which have come to mean the world to me. Scarred letters symbolic of my bond with her.

As if reading my mind, Azadeh turns and locks her deep brown eyes with mine. Those eyes are so enchanting. I could drown in their depths.

She smiles. "Pass me my knife."

I retrieve her sheath from her dresser and remove a sharp blade before handing it to her.

Azadeh steps away from Lev but leaves the gun in his ass. "Roll over, Lev."

Lev cautiously moves until his back is on the mattress. His cock stands straight up, pointing to the ceiling.

"You mean it? You're in this?" Azadeh asks, standing above him.

"Yes," Lev whispers.

"Tie him up," Cyrus says, pulling the rope from his kit and tossing it to me.

I don't know when he sneaked in his fire kit. Guess I was too fascinated with his Persian lollipop antics to notice.

244

I grab the rope and pull Azadeh's pistol from Lev's ass, handing it to her. "Move up the bed, Lev."

Pride blooms in me when Lev doesn't hesitate at the command. We've come a long way from the boy who never wanted to be touched to the man willing to relinquish control.

"You okay with this?" I ask, holding up the rope.

"I think so," Lev whispers.

"Remember, if you are uncomfortable, say your safe word, and it all stops. Everything."

Lev's steely eyes search mine. "It'll be okay."

Cyrus approaches Lev, his green eyes igniting as he lights the fire stick—a metal rod with a Kevlar white tip.

Once Lev is secure, feet tied to the footboard and hands to the headboard, Cyrus dabs yellow liquid on Lev's body with a pen.

"Why is it yellow?" I ask Cyrus.

"I wanted the three of you to know what I was writing. I used turmeric for food coloring."

Three words.

Mine.

Ours.

Yours.

Cyrus ignites each word with the torch and wipes it away. This is his way of fully embracing Lev. Once he's done, he extinguishes the torch and brushes his lips to Lev's in a sweet kiss. "Welcome home, Levinston. We've been waiting for you."

Cyrus turns to Azadeh. "All yours, Princess."

"That was beautiful in a very Cyrus-like way," Azadeh says as she jumps on the bed. She squats and grabs Lev's cock, lining it up with her entrance.

Lev moans as she sits on his dick. "Fuck," he growls, tugging at his wrists. He gazes up at Azadeh and growls. "I want to touch you."

"Azadeh and Cyrus have wanted to touch you for ten years. Now you know what we all went through." I slide my dick alongside his, pushing slowly until I'm snug inside Azadeh.

"I'm so not being left out." Cyrus moves behind me and forces me to kneel on the bed behind Azadeh. He cuts the rope and places Lev's feet on my shoulders. "Open up, fuck boy. Daddy has a treat for you. If you do a fantastic job and milk my cock nice and hard, it'll give you a creamy treat."

The three of us fuck Lev's holes as Azadeh pricks his skin with her knife. Blood trickles from his skin as she works to carve the letters into his flesh.

AZADEH.

The name of the angel who saved us and gave us a family. A mark all three of us now wear with pride and love.

Azadeh lowers her head to lap at the blood.

"I love you," Lev whispers. "I love all of you."

"We love you too, Lev," Azadeh says, her hands on Lev as if she can't get enough of touching him. "No matter what, we'll always love you."

I nip at Azadeh's ear, my teeth marring her delicate flesh. "I wasn't kidding about those babies, Princess. We're going to fuck this pretty cunt daily until you're pregnant. Every day, you'll walk around with our cum dripping out of this perfect cunt. When we tell you to get naked and spread your legs, you'll do it. We're going to fuck and breed you. That's all you're gonna do from now on. No more running off. This is your place now. Our queen, our wife, our fuckin' life." I cup her breasts and twist her pert nipples, making her scream as I pull her large breasts from her body. "Got it?"

"Yes," Azadeh moans.

"I love fucking my pretty pussy with Lev. You're always tight, but this is something else." Fuck. This is the only woman who's ever driven me mad. The only woman I've ever loved and ever will love. "I've loved you from the moment I saw you, Az." I pebble kisses along her shoulder. "You're going to be a good girl and be our free-use doll, aren't you, Princess?"

"Yes."

Lev comes first. He groans, and I feel his cum spurt from the tip of his cock. "That's it, Lev. Be a good boy and give her all that cum."

"Fuck, I can't hold off anymore. I'm gonna put a load in this hot ass. Shit, Lev. This fuck hole is nice and tight on my cock. I'm gonna have to fuck this ass daily. I'll put a load in Hellcat in the morning and you at night. I like the idea of you leaking my cum from this little ass." The bed shakes as Cyrus thrusts roughly into Lev. "Take my dick, slut. Milk my cock like the good little ass slut you are."

Azadeh bursts out laughing. "Milk my cock like the good little ass slut you are?" She pushes back against me and pulls my head down.

Cyrus grabs Azadeh by the throat. "You're talking too much, slut. Shut the fuck up and come."

His hand on her throat ignites Azadeh's release, and she stiffens as her pussy clamps around our cocks. She doesn't stop bouncing up and down as we push in and out until the three of us scream our orgasm in unison.

"Pull out of her, Zeke," Cyrus demands. "I want to watch that cum drip into my new fuck toy's mouth."

I reluctantly pull out of Azadeh, and she rises to stand over Lev's face.

"Open that pathetic mouth of yours, Lev. Nice and wide. I want to make sure you catch every drop." Cyrus kneels behind Lev and lowers his head to his ass. "Clean up our girl's holes while I lick your ass clean."

I'm surprised when my cock rises as I witness the cum drip from Azadeh's into Lev's waiting mouth while Cyrus's tongue deeps into Lev's ass and sucks out all the cum he's emptied there.

Cyrus turns to me and smirks. "You can lube up my ass, Daddy. I think I'd like to see Lev take another load in his mouth."

I smirk as I grab the lube, pouring it on my cock before I grip Cyrus's ass and pound into him. "I told you I was the top, and you're the bottom. How does it feel to know you'll always be a nice wet cunt for me to fuck?"

Cyrus laughs. "Usually, I'd have you on the floor for that, but I'm feeling pretty fuckin' high on life right now."

Once we're finished and everyone has come multiple times, I turn on the shower, and the four of us load into it. Unlike the dirty nature of our fucking, these touches are kind, caring, and full of compassion.

Cyrus has Lev pinned against the wall, a cloth moving gently on his cock and asshole while he kisses Lev and whispers how much he loves him.

I thread my hands through Azadeh's hair, massaging the conditioner in her silky black locks.

"I wasn't joking about the babies," I whisper. "I want them."

She turns and wraps her arms around my neck. "And I want to give them to you."

Epilogue

Azadeh Ten Years Later

I sit in the gazebo built for me many years ago as the kids run like wild animals in the yard, chased by two men who are just as wild.

The four of us married nine years ago in a makeshift civil ceremony. Obviously, it wasn't legally binding, but we wanted something symbolic to show the world our commitment to each other.

We started weekly therapy sessions to work out our trauma. I was adamant about not bringing children into this world until we had a better coping mechanism to deal with our issues than sex. The guys agreed, and we've been attending weekly therapy sessions since as a family. Our daughter Nasrin was born two years later, followed by our twin boys two years later.

I gave up my journeys around the globe, but Lev set up a non-profit that I run, which helps girls who need to escape bad situations. We've saved five thousand girls from dire conditions in the eight years it's been running.

"I never thought this place would be my refuge," Lev says, wrapping his arms around me and rubbing my pregnant belly. Our next child is due in a month. "Never thought the place of nightmares would become the place of perfect dreams."

"We have a good life, Lev," I say, bringing his left hand to my lips. His wedding band shines in the sunlight.

Lev kisses my cheek, watching our two men and three kids play. "We sure do."

Thank you for reading Feral. The next book in the Darkly Ever After Series is Obsession and you can pre order it Here

About the Author

http://www.authormilacrawford.com/

If you Enjoyed This Book You Might Also Enjoy

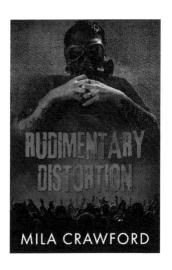

We were the kids of addicts, discarded and forgotten about by the people who were supposed to love us the most. But together we found family and created our own solace. I never thought I would be alone because I had them. Until one night changed everything.

The world knows them as Satan and Blaze. The masked lead singer and drummer of international rock sensation Gutless Void.

I know them as Lars Morgan and Cain Foster. The two boys I loved who broke my heart.

Manufactured by Amazon.ca
Bolton, ON